EARL OF SHEFFORD

MAKE MINE AN EARL SERIES
BOOK 3

ANNA ST CLAIRE
USA TODAY BESTSELLING AUTHOR

EARL OF SHEFFORD
PUBLISHED BY: SASSY ROMANCES

Copyright © 2021 by Anna St. Claire
All rights reserved.

Cover Design by Joanna D'Angelo
Edited by John Polsom-Jenkins,
Safeword Author Services

For My Granddaughters,

. . . who at their young ages don't understand why Mimi is always writing.

*It is my fondest hope that each of you discovers a love that feels like
friendship to music—
as I have found in my own life.*

~Love Mimi

CHAPTER 1

LONDON, ENGLAND ~ SEPTEMBER 1822

"*T*hat, I believe, is the game!" Colin Nelson, the Earl of Shefford, breathed a sigh of relief. How had Bergen talked him into one more game with Lord Wilford Whitton? He already suspected the man cheated when he could, and failing that, he was a terrible loser. Tonight, the man could not cover his losses without giving up some part of his estate, having already lost both his horse and a building. A building, indeed, which now belonged to Colin, even though he was uncertain of what it looked like or its actual worth. *Nevertheless, I plan to put it to good use*, he mused. *Hell and confound it! The paper feels damp.* He glanced at the vowel before tucking it into his waistcoat pocket—making sure Whitton's perspiration had not smeared the ink before wiping his hands on his pantaloons.

"My lord, might we exchange a few words about this for a moment? Perhaps there is another way to pay you. The building has been in my family for a long while." Lord Whitton grabbed his chewed, cold cigar, which had been resting next to his empty glass, and stood up from the table. The short, red-faced lord had been huffing since he had shown his losing cards. "I have an idea and I think you might be interested in my proposal."

"I cannot imagine what else you could have. You have already wagered your horse and lost it; and now, this family building. I do not make a habit of leaving women and children homeless by winning a man's house from him." He watched Whitton wipe the sweat from his head. By now, that handkerchief had to be soaked, he thought, trying to decide how to handle the man who was growing more and more fidgety. Instinct told him it was time to leave. "I have no notion whether this building is worth the hundred pounds you owe me, but I know the area and will take a chance." Colin pushed back from the table and stood up. "The game is over. I suggest you go home." He looked around the room. Circles of cigar smoke hovered over several heads before making its way to the general haze of smoke at the ceiling. Activity ceased at the closest tables, as the players' heads turned to watch. Even the popping and crackling from the enormous fireplace across the room seemed louder and closer. He found himself buoyed by the temporary audience.

"If you will, please hear me out." Perspiration coated the man's forehead. "I should not have wagered the building."

"Yet you did," Colin responded coolly. "The gaming table has not been kind to you this night. Perhaps you should have stopped playing after you lost your horse to Lord Bergen." People like Whitton would benefit from house limits on wagers, yet they rarely put one in place.

"I thought I could win back my losses. 'Twas but a small debt," the man whined. "My horse is a thoroughbred. It should have carried me further on the wager."

Colin noted the tone of indignation steeling Whitton's voice. "Yet you lost that to a different person," Colin said with a note of astonishment even he could hear.

"He is your *friend*. How do I know the two of you have played fair?" The man sneered, the accusation clear.

From the corner of his eye, Colin observed his friend, Thomas, the Earl of Bergen, quietly signal the stalwart individual standing beside the door with a nod of his head. The last thing they needed was to dive into a mill in this hell. Colin was already regretting the decision to try out this new hell. They should have gone to the club. He did not care for public displays.

"I will give you one chance to redeem your building. If you can satisfy your entire debt by tomorrow evening—*in cash*—I will return the deed to the building. If not, consider the building payment in full."

A tall, burly man with dark hair and a trimmed beard appeared at the table. "My lord, the night has ended for you. We ask that you leave now," the bouncer said, his eyes on Whitton. For added emphasis, he pushed up each of his sleeves, revealing large, muscular arms. A tattoo of an ace of spades with a dagger across it showed on the underside of one arm.

"They have cheated me," Whitton accused, pointing a finger at Bergen and Shefford. "These are the gentlemen you should throw out —and I demand the return of the deed he stole from me," he rasped, taking a step back.

"Did you just call me a cheat?" Colin stepped forward, his voice low.

The bouncer grabbed Lord Whitton by the back of his coat. "My lord, there are windows throughout the house. If there was any cheating occurring, we would see it. I will escort you to the door. Your participation for the evening—*here, at least*—is over." With that, the guard forcibly removed the squirming, protesting man.

"You have not heard the last of me," Whitton yelled over his shoulder, before being dragged to the door.

"Well, that did not end too well," observed Colin, quietly. "I hope he finds his way home."

"Without his horse," sneered Bergen.

"Do you think he will try to take his horse? He lost it to you," Colin added wryly.

"I conjured that he might and removed the horse to the stable across the street, with ours, when I took a break from the tables earlier. I am glad I insisted on a signed bill of sale."

"Ah. Yes, that was probably wise," Colin quipped.

"Faro does not appear to be his game, Shefford," Bergen said, taking the last sip of his brandy. "Mm, I think this must be French brandy. How unusual to find it at a gaming hell." He sniffed the rim of the glass and smiled, as if confirming his point.

"I feel the need for more salubrious surroundings. What say you we head to the club?"

"That *is* funny! I am right behind you, my friend." Bergen sniggered. He picked up his coat and followed Colin.

As the two men approached the stable, a young man jumped up from where he was sitting, beneath a tree near the gate.

"M'lords," he started, brushing off his breeches. "Can I bring yer horses to ye?"

"This is the young man who has been taking care of my winnings tonight," Bergen said, chuckling.

"Me name's Danny. I'm glad to see ye, m'lord," the young man rejoined. "A shorter gentleman came fer that horse, just like ye said. I 'ad placed her in the back, in case I was with another when 'e came. He was really mad when I told him ye had taken her."

"That was good thinking. Here is a little something extra for watching our horses and being so thoughtful, Danny," Colin said, withdrawing the money from his waistcoat.

"Get away! A crown. You gents are the dog's whiskers!"

"We had a run of luck at the tables tonight and our good fortune has become your gain," Bergen added, grinning.

"Thank you," the lad said with gusto. "I'll be back in a jiffy with the horses." He pocketed the coin and hurried into the stables.

"It is interesting how Whitton's demeanor changed so rapidly," Bergen remarked thoughtfully. "You should beware. A loser's remorse can do strange things to a body. Perhaps I should apologize for talking you into one more game."

"There is no need. I won." Colin grinned. "Although I will admit I do not understand the building's worth. It could have the walls eaten through and be overrun with rats, for all I know. I plan to take a look in a day or so—if he does not find the readies for his debt."

"That was a very generous offer. You were more than fair."

"Here come our horses." Colin never felt comfortable with compliments, no matter how sincere. "I merely gave him an opportunity. The old codger seemed abnormally worried about the loss of the building."

"What are you thinking to do with a building you have yet to see, Colin?" Bergen asked, his tone one of amusement.

"Ah! Here are the horses," he said again in an attempt to deflect his friend's attention. He had an idea for the building but preferred to speak to his brother first. "It would seem our return will be slower... I suspect you will have to pull along the second horse." He eyed the mare with disfavor. "It was very well of you to move her..." Colin let his voice fade as he noticed the boy's face. Something was wrong. The hair on the back of his neck prickled. He turned around, just in time to block Lord Whitton's knife as the man thrust it towards his back. Colin's right arm received the punishing blow instead, but ignoring the pain, he pummeled Whitton with both fists, knocking him off balance. Shouting to Danny to run for help, Bergen joined him, and the two men wrestled Whitton to the ground.

"You should have that looked at," Bergen observed some minutes later as they watched a pair of constables lead Lord Whitton away in handcuffs to the lock-up. "I have never seen that man so out of control. Attacking a peer—whatever next?" He grimaced. "I cannot imagine what drove him to do such a thing."

"I will speak with the magistrate on that situation tomorrow. I have a disquieting feeling about that gentleman, and I need to make sure that they punish him for the assault," Colin muttered. "Can you help me onto my horse?"

"I will. However, I insist you come to my house. I will send for the doctor. The cut is deep and needs to be attended."

"Very well. However, I wish you will not make too much of it," Colin returned, grimacing in the other direction. *Distraction could help.* His arm felt on fire. "I would like to speak with Baxter about Whitton and make sure that he does not escape justice."

"Yes, indeed."

"Hopefully, the magistrate will send him to gaol, and they keep him there for a goodly while," Bergen added.

"He can rot there," Colin returned. "The man is dangerous and should not be among decent folk."

"He is obviously in quite deep. Unless someone owes *him*, he is not likely to have enough blunt to grease the gaoler's fist," agreed Bergen. "Whitton may be a scoundrel; however, he is also an earl. I will send word to Baxter and Morray once I have you safely home. The sooner he is under lock and key, the better."

CHAPTER 2

*H*onoria Mason glanced about the room, taking in the sleeping faces of fourteen children. *My little angels.* The room still smelled of paint and lye soap, despite her efforts to air it, yet it was an affirmation of the level of cleanliness she demanded. The school reopened three months hence, and these small children had already claimed their places. All of the children were ten years of age or under, with one toddler—a little girl. Since they did not have older children, they had made the decision to put them all in the largest room, while the painting and repairs continued in the others. Too soon, they would need the other rooms. For now, it was nice to see them all together.

One small iron crib and thirteen wooden beds lined opposing walls. A small iron sconce held a single candle that flickered from the wall on which it hung, away from the bedding. The dim light it provided was barely enough to see all the children's faces from the doorway. Lately, Nora had wondered about the women who might not have cast their children away had they had some financial help. Merely surviving, financially, was out of reach for many of these women without support.

Nora herself did not have money, but she had space and she had some connections. Much though she reviled the *ton*, perhaps there were some situations in which they could help others less fortunate. She needed to give the idea more thought. While she would never understand how someone could cast off their child, no matter the circumstances, she was open-minded enough to know that everyone did not fit that mold. Society saw many of them as unworthy and, in some cases, by-blows to be hidden away from view.

Parents or relatives of these children had abandoned them here or on the streets, unable or unwilling to care for them. They often cast the children out without a look back, something which broke her heart to even think of. Others lost their parents through disease or worse and were left with nowhere to turn. To remain on the street would only lead to them becoming pawns of the pickpocket gangs, who taught them to steal. It was important that these cherubs learn a respectable trade, one which would place them away from danger. She did not wish for Society to have so much control that they had no choices in life, Nora reflected, realizing with surprising clarity she was thinking of her own situation.

"Och! They are quiet at last." A voice spoke behind her, startling her from her thoughts.

"Yes, you are right, Mrs. Simpkins," she murmured, her mind still trying to grasp the notion that perhaps the *ton* itself could help undo some misfortune she saw in front of her. Nora was no fool. Some of these children were bastards, born out of wedlock to women who, perhaps because of their positions within a household or Society, could not keep a child. These women could ill afford to lose their positions and had few resources to use. *How difficult that must be*, she thought, *to choose.*

"I ken ye well enough to see ye are thinking about something serious," the older woman whispered. "It does me heart good to see how much like yer grandma that ye be."

Perceiving only benefits from her ideas, Nora determined to list them and visit her benefactor—Grandmama. She needed more than money to make some changes she envisioned.

"I feel as though I am taking advantage, yet my grandmother has often urged me to apply to her whenever I have need of anything," returned Nora.

"Nay. Ye do not ken how proud she is of ye." After a moment of silence, Mrs. Simpkins smiled and added, "I do not hear the wee one that came today. Perhaps that is a good sign."

It was not unusual for the new children to cry themselves to sleep for several nights upon their arrival. She and Mrs. Simpkins worked hard to soothe the transition. Nora was thankful that her grandmother had loaned her the older cook—who constantly showed a heart of gold towards the children. Three women—herself, Mrs. Simpkins, and Mary, the maid—made up the household. In addition, Mr. Marsh, Grandmama's gardener and handyman, came twice a week to help with the land and any jobs that might require a man's strength.

Nora's means were barely sufficient, and while bread and soup had become a staple, she had found Mrs. Simpkins to be a genius at making a sumptuous meal for the children from only a few supplies. Nora refused to take more money from her grandmother than necessary.

A cry came then from a toddler in the corner, and Nora rushed over. "There, there, Amy. I am here, little one."

"Mama," the child wailed, and then coughed repeatedly.

An older child raised her head. "I think she misses her mama, Miss Nora. She can sleep next to me, if that'll help."

"Alice, that is very sweet of you. I think I will walk about with Amy for a few minutes." She leaned over and kissed the six-year-old girl on the forehead. "Go back to sleep, little one."

"Thank you, Miss Nora." The child had barely whispered her response when soft snores came from her cot.

Turning to the crib, Nora took a deep breath and out of habit, smoothed her skirt with her hands. "This transition will be hard for you, little one." She reached into the cradle, picked up the whimpering child, and held her to her chest, to comfort her.

"There, there, fret not, little one. We will look after you," she cooed to the little girl.

Mrs. Simpkins met her at the door. "I remembered we had a little of this left over and thought warm goat's milk could help."

"Thank you, Mrs. Simpkins. It may take both of us to help her recover from her grief. It never ceases to amaze me that people consider children as chattel. They have hearts and feelings. I will take her to my room and rock her to sleep. I should probably have a small bed installed in the corner for times such as these," she added.

"'Tis not a bad idea. Remember, I am here if ye need me, Miss Nora. I will care for the children as if they were me own," the woman responded.

"I know you will. You are a good, thoughtful woman, and you always made my visits to Grandmama better when I was a child. I do not recall that your lemon biscuits ever hurt me," Nora said warmly as she kissed the toddler on the head. Mrs. Simpkins' kind heart was one reason that Grandmama had lent her to the school. The thought forced a smile to bubble up. She had long ago recognized her maternal grandmother as having a kindred soul to her own, and often, she had not even had to ask before Grandmama had responded with what was needed.

"The wee one has only been here a day. Give her time. She is strong." Mrs. Simpkins gently squeezed the little girl's hand and kissed her on the cheek.

Little Amy had arrived yesterday, and already the tiny, amber-haired toddler threatened to steal Nora's heart. A friend of the child's mother had delivered her. Circumstances forced Amy's mother into prostitution to survive and she had died of syphilis. Nora knew little about the disease, it not being a subject considered suitable for young ladies. However, she understood it was a horrible death. She shuddered, recalling the moment the child arrived. The woman who brought Amy handed the crying child to Nora at the door.

"I wrote everything I knew about her on the note in her bundle," the woman said, pointing to the knotted shawl sitting on the step. "I would keep her, but I know naught about children. Her mother loved Amy very much. She was a kind woman who did what she must to survive. Please—you will find me if I can help Amy?" she said, brushing away tears. "She knows me as Auntie Gemma," the woman added before turning and rushing down the street, clearly eager to distance herself from the task she had undertaken.

The small child's story made Nora's eyes mist as she recollected it and, out of instinct, she pulled the child closer to her own heart. Nora knew that each child in the room had a story equally sad, and she could not allow herself to dissolve into tears with each one. These children needed strength and permanence. She would work hard to give them that. If her idea had merit, it could help some children to stay with their mothers. Buoyed by her thoughts, she looked around once more.

The orphanage which had once occupied the building had closed about ten years past. Although Grandmama owned the building, she had not had the will to open it again, as Grandpapa had died about the same time. Eager to assist those 'thrown on the parish', Nora had found a willing partner in her grandmother, and felt fortunate to have talked her family into reopening the building—although her uncle had threatened to sell it on many occasions, citing its uselessness. According to Aunt Sophie, they were at low water because of his gambling debts. She would be exceedingly worried if Uncle controlled the property, yet she need not be concerned. Papa had informed her shortly after her grandmother discussed reopening the orphanage, that Grandmama owned the property, as it had been part of her wedding portion. *Thank goodness, Grandmama holds the deed to this building.*

The whimpering stopped at last as the small child stilled in her arms, content to sleep. Deciding to let the child sleep, Nora walked to her room and took a chair in the corner, careful not to disturb Amy. She leaned back in the chair and closed her eyes, suddenly over-whelmed with her own need for sleep.

CHAPTER 3

TWO DAYS LATER

Free of the fever caused by the knife wound, and healed sufficiently, Colin determined he needed fresh air. He intended to take advantage of the clear London skies this morning presented. Adjusting his waistcoat, he withdrew the folded paper from his pocket, shaking it open. Finally! Here was a chance to set the wheels in motion for the fencing club he and his brother had talked about for years. Winning this building had become a prompt in his mind to make it happen. He would have the building renovated to his brother's specifications and Jonathan would run it. He was the expert in the *duello*. Their father had encouraged the skill, often sparring with his sons. Colin considered himself more than proficient at the art of fencing; however, Jonathan's skill was far beyond mere competence. He almost equaled the legendary Angelo.

Besides, Colin reasoned, he was much too busy to run a club. He had taken the bet on faith, being previously unaware of the building's existence, let alone having knowledge of its condition. Upon reflection, there had been little—if not naught—trustworthy about Wilford Whitton. The nasty knife wound in his own arm, which was still in danger of infection, was proof of that. However, he could no longer tolerate staring at the four walls of his room.

Still involved with the Crown, and now with his estate, Colin found fencing an excellent way of releasing pent-up emotion and helping him to feel bobbish. He felt sure this entertainment would also be a welcome diversion within his set at the Wicked Earl's Club. The gentlemen met almost nightly, and no matter the requirement for amusement, the club could, for the most part, meet it. As yet, it had not provided a fencing saloon.

The sport itself had diminished somewhat in status, overtaken by the popularity of shooting; however, it remained an effective and punishing method of defense that, if vigorously practiced, kept a gentleman's body at peak performance.

Caught up in the excitement of his thoughts, he picked up his cane and whipped it into a parry at an imaginary opponent—only to be immediately reminded of the stitches he had received only two days ago.

His arm ached, and that Whitton had caused it pricked his pride. He should have been more careful, expecting something from the man. He pulled out his pocket watch, mindful that Bergen and Lord Morray were meeting with him soon.

Where was Joseph? His valet was taking an inordinate amount of time to find a suitable coat. He fingered the frilled cuffs of his shirt distractedly. The man had pursed his lips anxiously when the bandage around Colin's upper arm did not easily fit inside the brown wool coat he had chosen for today and had hurried from the room, muttering about fetching one with a better fit. Some minutes earlier, he had informed Colin that his black coat had been returned, repaired by his tailor. Presumably, therefore, the man had gone to fetch the garment.

Colin turned his head at the slight knock at the door. "Come in."

"My lord, I apologize for the delay. I took the liberty of remeasuring the arm openings, in order to compare them with the brown coat. They are just as required and should provide room for your injury. It has also been cleaned."

"God's teeth, man! I was wondering where you had gone. I had hoped to view an investment before meeting with my brother." Colin stretched his arms into the sleeves as Joseph fussed with the shoulders. "It looks better than new. Thank you, Joseph," he acknowledged in a milder tone. The black coat would suit for what he needed to do today.

Joseph was the grandson of his father's valet and had proven himself more than capable. The man had become indispensable in the three years he had been in his service.

"Mr. Weston has attached a new sleeve," Joseph responded abstractedly, still twitching with the back.

Colin wanted to set out. "Have the footman summon my carriage to be brought around, if you will."

"I anticipated your need, my lord. The carriage is already at the front, awaiting your convenience," Joseph said, smiling. "Lord Bergen has arrived and is waiting in the drawing room."

"Your ability to predict my requirements never ceases to amaze me, Joseph."

"It is merely a part of my duties, my lord. I apologize for not considering the need to accommodate your bandage."

"Think naught of it," Colin responded, suddenly feeling guilty about the way he had spoken to the young valet. The lanky young man that shadowed his grandfather in those last years of the older man's service had matured into a fine young man. Tall, with blond hair, broad shoulders, and bright blue eyes, he was a favorite among Colin's staff. Surprisingly, it was more for his willingness to help anyone that needed an extra pair of hands than his masculine stature. "Thank you, Joseph."

Humming to himself, Colin grabbed his cane and joined his friend downstairs. Adam Beaumont, the Earl of Morray had not yet arrived. The Earl was the one gentleman in Colin's set he had counted upon to give him a realistic idea of the popularity of the venture he had in mind. He was not only a friend, but a frequent sparring partner at Jackson's Saloon. His opinion on both the location and the popularity of the investment meant a great deal to Colin.

Less than an hour later, his coachman pulled the town chariot into a short, circular drive. Colin and his two friends stepped out of the carriage and stared up at a three-story, faded pink building surrounded by iron railings on a corner, northeast of Mayfair. Russell Square was a respectable if not fashionable neighborhood, yet not considered a dangerous one. He did not wish customers to be set upon by riff-raff. He found it was close enough to his prospective clients, while far enough removed for discretion. The location pleased him.

"Not a bad locality," he remarked, hoping to spur his friends' opinions. An instant later, he thought he saw movement in a window and squinted. *Are those curtains? It looks inhabited. According to Whitton, this was supposed to be an empty building.*

"I thought you had mentioned the building being empty. Unless my eyes deceive me, I saw a woman's face—a rather charming woman's face—in that upper window," Morray said, pointing to the large second-floor window, centrally placed above the door.

"Then I was not seeing things," Colin retorted in some chagrin. He regarded Bergen, who stood next to him, smiling, having not uttered a word.

Colin prompted Bergen with a slight nudge of his elbow. "He said the building was empty, did he not?" he queried.

"He did. However, he also tried to weasel out of the bet. I am thinking the reasons he failed to share are currently residing in that building, and *she* has no notion she is being evicted. Unless my memory fails me, this used to be an orphanage before it closed some years ago." He eyed his friends. "Could it be that it has become so again? I say we should meet the young woman inside and find out. I would like to have a complete story to share with Elizabeth when I return home." He laughed sardonically.

Colin tried to be irritated with his friend, but he could lay nothing at Bergen's feet. He almost envied his friend. Bergen was happily married—something he could never achieve himself. He was uncertain he was even ready to consider marriage at this time. Thomas Bergen had married Lady Elizabeth Newton over five years ago, after discovering her living a quiet but remarkable life, caring for her children and abandoned animals. He had brought her an orphaned donkey he had found while on the way to London, having heard she adopted strays of all types. The donkey, Clarence, had found a home and his friend had found a wife he had not been seeking. Besides the three children she had already adopted, they had twins of their own— a boy and a girl. *Lucky fellow*, he thought irrationally.

"I cannot see the humor here," Colin said, irritated. This created a whole new wrinkle in his quest to help his brother. He pulled out the deed and glanced first at a brass sign attached to the railings and then back to the deed. "We have the right of it. Shall we find out what more there is to this story?" It incensed him to be caught like a flat through accepting a chance wager.

"You should probably determine the legitimacy of the paper he gave you," Morray added in a droll tone. "Yet we are here. I propose we meet the chit and find out what we can."

Morray was always willing to *meet the chit*, Colin thought miserably. "She occupies my property and is *not* grist for your mill, Morray. This may very well be an orphanage." Even to his own ear, he sounded testy. Perhaps it was the combination of being injured and swindled. He had thought things might not be as Whitton represented, and rather than follow his intuition, he succumbed to the lure of the game. Winning the building presented a suitable solution to his and Jonathan's desire to honor their father.

Morray snorted. "Ownership remains to be seen, but fear not, my fine fellow. You *know* innocent ladies are not to my taste. I prefer, shall I say, a more savage entertainment. Your young woman is safe."

"She is not my woman," Colin snapped.

"I say, Shefford, you are letting this become bothersome. I have found that the biggest surprises can sometimes turn out to be the best ones. I, for one, am eager to meet the face behind the curtain." Morray jerked his head towards the same curtain which had moved earlier, revealing a lovely face framed by soft, blonde ringlets staring down at the three of them.

The large oak door at the top of the steps had recently been rubbed down, most likely to prepare for a fresh coat of paint. Colin took in the neatened appearance of the portico and lifted the plain brass knocker to announce their presence. Less than a minute later, a small hatch above the knocker slid open and an older woman's face appeared for a moment before the opening closed and the door opened.

"Good day, my lords. May I be of help?" A short, mob-capped woman stood at the door, filling the opening.

"I am Lord Shefford, and I wish to look over my recently acquired property. I must admit to being somewhat startled to find the house occupied," Colin began.

"Oh, dear! Beg pardon, my lord." The short woman closed the door.

"I say, did you just get the door closed in your face?" Bergen gibed.

"Stubble it, Bergen." He lifted the knocker and gave three quick raps.

"I am sorry, Shefford. I should not be fooling at your expense." Bergen smirked, putting the lie to his apology. "'Tis just that this reminds me a little of my first meeting with Elizabeth. I think I am merely amused by the coincidence."

"This has no similarity to when you met your wife, I assure you. I am not meeting my future wife," he grumbled as the door opened again. The older woman had disappeared, replaced by a beautiful young woman dressed in a plain cotton dress of a deep navy-blue color, covered with a white apron. She had golden blonde hair, bound neatly in a loose chignon, and chocolate brown eyes—eyes a man could lose himself in. "May I speak with your employer, my dear," Colin said politely.

"Good day, my lords." She bobbed a curtsey. "My name is Miss Mason and I am the headmistress here. Please forgive my housekeeper's lack of deference." She paused, smiling sweetly. "We are unaccustomed to having many visitors, especially gentlemen as distinguished as yourselves. Have you come to make a donation to the school?"

CHAPTER 4

*N*ora could not imagine why these three gentlemen—obviously members of the *ton*, judging by their dress and means of transport—had remained standing in front of her school for what seemed like an eternity. They were all dressed in the height of fashion, with superfine coats sporting high collars, pantaloons, white linen shirts, colorful silk waistcoats, and elaborately tied cravats. She watched them chatting among themselves until they finally approached the door. She had hoped they would leave. While two men were dressed in navy and burgundy jackets with buff pants, the tallest one was dressed in black, which she thought was an unusual color for this time of day. When that tall, dark-headed man with soft grey eyes unfurled a folded piece of paper and looked up at her, her stomach both fluttered and sank to her feet, a curious feeling she failed to understand. Perhaps it was a premonition. Various people acquainted with the family had told her that her mother had been subject to them; however, Nora made it a practice to follow her instincts, and they told her something was wrong here. Whatever the gentlemen's reasons, she remained on her guard as she greeted them, forcing a smile and the cheery voice she employed whenever she felt worried and fearful. The gentleman took a moment to take her measure and take stock of the room behind her before speaking.

"I fear there has been some mistake. Would you be so kind as to invite us inside to discuss it?" he finally said. "I should hate my business to be discussed by eavesdroppers and passers-by."

She had to admit several wagons, and people on foot had slowed down or even stopped to watch. This was a busy street, yet not one accustomed to gentlemen of such style and fashion. She nodded in agreement.

"You have me at a disadvantage, my lord," she returned, noticing that the other two had remained quiet and observant. He seemed in charge.

"It would appear my shock has stolen my manners, Miss Mason. Forgive me. I am the Earl of Shefford." He made an elegant leg before continuing, "The gentleman to my right is my friend, the Earl of Bergen, and to the left of me is the Earl of Morray." Both men removed their beaver hats and bowed.

Chagrined that not only was this gentleman being too nice to dislike, he was also remarkably attractive. Nora stepped back and allowed them entry.

"The parlor is to the left," she directed them, pausing a moment to speak with her cook, who had remained standing quietly at the foot of the stairs. "Mrs. Simpkins," she whispered to the older woman, "please ask Mary to bring us some tea."

"Aye, though I be glad to do it for ye, missy, Mary is quieting Amy just now. The poor lass refuses to nap," the cook replied. "I be afraid she has adopted ye for her mama," she added with a rueful smile. "She has taken a likin' to ye for sure."

Poor little Amy. She had not forgotten the child, although she had become very distracted by the appearance of these gentlemen.

"I am afraid you may well be correct," she said with a sigh. "If you do not mind bringing a tray to the parlor, I would appreciate it. You are a treasure, Mrs. Simpkins."

"I'll add some fresh lemon biscuits I jus' took from the oven. That should help with whatever trouble awaits ye," she murmured. With a curt nod to the dark-haired, grey-eyed man who stared in their direction through the open door, the older woman left to gather the promised refreshments.

Nora pushed the door behind her towards its frame, leaving it open a crack. Instinct told her that whatever business they had, the children should not hear of it.

"Gentlemen, I have requested tea for us." She walked over to a somewhat worn, blue velvet settee and sat down. "Please make yourselves comfortable, and once again, I trust you will accept my apologies for earlier. I should perhaps explain… you have caught us at an awkward time. We are still establishing our routines. The orphanage has just reopened after being closed for ten years, you see. There is much to repair and I have yet to appoint a porter."

"*Orphanage?*" the Earl mouthed to his friends as he took his seat in a yellow and blue patterned chair next to a matching blue sofa. Although her grandmother had insisted, she was tired of the colors, Nora was well aware it was a Banbury story. She could not refuse without appearing ungrateful and, truth be known, she had been very glad to accept, for it meant she had one respectable room in which to receive guests,

The other two men quietly retired to a small, round maple table with two matching chairs. Turning the chairs towards Nora and Lord Shefford, they sat down.

"Permit me to beg your pardon for the intrusion, Miss Mason. We thought the building was unoccupied. I wish to inspect it with a view to its suitability for another use entirely. You can imagine my surprise," Lord Shefford responded, his voice echoing disbelief.

"Then I think we must both be thunderstruck by these events," she said, forcing her lips into a stiff smile. "My family has fully supported my efforts to reopen the orphanage which closed, as I informed you earlier, ten years past. I am trying to understand how it can be possible you thought the property to be available," she added sweetly, trusting the tremors in her voice were hidden beneath the strength of her words. Uncle's threat to sell resonated in her head. *Surely Grandmama did not agree to that. There has to be a mistake.* Her heart pounded.

"I can only apologize again for thrusting business upon you," Lord Shefford replied, "but I think this document will convey everything."

Nora studied the paper. It appeared to be a deed to the building, signed by Uncle Wilford.

"How can this be? I have been told that my uncle does not own the rights to this building. My grandmother does."

"Perhaps he has been placed in charge of her possessions," Lord Shefford offered.

"I hesitate to disagree with you, sir, but my grandfather purchased this building as a gift for my grandmother. She recently encouraged me to reopen the orphanage." Nora took a deep breath and tried to quiet her nerves. "I fear there has been a dreadful mistake," she continued.

"I hardly think so, Miss Mason. Your uncle used this deed to cover a wager in a game of chance two evenings ago. He lost. The building is mine." He gazed about the room. "I did not understand the property was occupied..." He paused. "I have no wish to turn women and small children out of their home. Therefore, with your forbearance, I should like a few days to consider an alternative for you."

Nora wanted to scream, but training dictated she remain as calm as possible, no matter how boorish this man was being. It was all of a piece and joined the other reasons she hated the *ton*—its members only thought of themselves. Her family had lost too much. *She* had lost too much. She would not lose this building. Her children would not lose their home.

"With all due respect, my lord, there has been a mistake. This building is owned by my grandmother. If she had given it to my uncle to *manage*..." She nearly spat the word. "...she would have informed me, as she has been assisting me with the reopening." Silence fell over the room, broken only by the ticking of the long-case clock in one corner. Nora tried not to fidget with her hands where they lay folded in her lap. What could she say? The faces of the three gentlemen gave no clue as to their thoughts.

A slight knock on the door heralded the entrance of Mrs. Simpkins with the tea tray. Nora was never more glad to see anyone in her life.

"Thank you, Mrs. Simpkins," Nora said, with more warmth than perhaps the service warranted. Then, stiffening her spine and smiling through clenched teeth, she addressed Lord Shefford. "My grandmother has also generously lent me her cook. Mrs. Simpkins has been kind enough to take on the role of cook-housekeeper for the school."

"Your grandmother's cook?" Lord Bergen spoke up from the back, ignoring the startled faces of his friends. "May I inquire who your grandmother is, Miss Mason?"

Nora took a deep breath. At least one of the three had a reasonable mind. She turned to Mrs. Simpkins.

"That will be all," she said firmly as Mrs. Simpkins showed a desire to linger.

"Very good, miss." Bobbing an unsteady curtsey, the cook reluctantly left the room.

Turning back to face the gentlemen, Nora's gaze met Lord Shefford's before she lowered it politely.

"I find this whole matter most distressing, but since, on this occasion, it is so important," she said, pausing, "I will tell you. My grandmother is the Dowager Countess of Whitton." She fought the smile that threatened to burst forth at the pale look on Lord Shefford's face. Doing her best to contain her glee at turning the tables on the arrogant earl, she smoothed out her dress before picking up her favorite cornflower blue porcelain teapot. "Tea, gentlemen?" she offered, as she began pouring the beverage and passing the filled cups to her astonished guests.

Each of the gentlemen sipped their tea, apparently lost in their own quiet contemplation. When Nora had finished the contents of her cup, she rose, forcing them also to stand.

"Gentlemen, I would greatly appreciate the chance to consult with my grandmother. She is due to visit later today." Adopting a look of utter puzzlement, she peered up at Lord Shefford. "My lord, I can only imagine how you must feel. Allow me to discuss this with my grandmother, for she may wish to consult with you regarding the signed deed."

"Ahem," he said, clearing his throat. "I apologize for my apparent rudeness. It was not meant. However, it would seem we have an unexpected tangle here. I will also engage my man of business to look into this matter further."

Lord Shefford returned his empty cup to the tray at the same time she moved the teapot and inadvertently, Nora touched his bare hand with her own. Quivers of feeling shot straight up her arm causing her to nearly jerk her hand away. She willed calmness over her body, puzzled over the something she had never before experienced. "Certainly, my lord," Nora choked out, startled when she caught herself staring—most improperly—into the gentleman's grey eyes. *Not that I would... yet if I could ever be accepted as a viable match for a gentleman of his standing, I would not mind one who looked as fine as he does.*

The soft telltale scuffle of footsteps in the hall interrupted her thoughts and drew her attention to the door. Unnoticed, Mrs. Simpkins had left it open to the room, giving some semblance of propriety. Meeting three men alone in her parlor had not been anticipated, and with minimal staff and no lady's maid, Mrs. Simpkins probably stood close enough to offer a chaperone's assistance. Despite initial frustration, she found herself appreciative of the older woman's efforts to add a level of decorum for reputation's sake.

When the three gentlemen had finally taken their leave, she leaned against the door and heaved a heavy sigh of relief. She realized it was only a reprieve. Surely, Grandmama would have some solution?

CHAPTER 5

"*W*ell, *that* did not proceed as I would have predicted," Bergen observed in a jovial voice. "By golly, though, I enjoyed her spunk!" he added as the three men made their way to the carriage.

"If I have followed this situation correctly, Lord Whitton has not only deceived his family, but he may also have forged a deed," Morray propounded. "I know the Countess to be quite a force among the *ton* —she differs greatly from her wastrel son."

"While it is best not to jump to conclusions, instinct tells me that Whitton has forged the deed. Still, I shall ask Thomas Yarrow, my man of business, to scrutinize it and advise me on a proper course of action." Colin stuffed the questionable deed into his pocket.

"A sound plan," agreed Bergen. "I bet Yarrow has come across such doings before—perhaps, even, with Whitton. It would be helpful to know."

"In our business, we have had dealings with a great number of rogues, but I have never encountered a peer forging a deed to cover his gambling debts. I cannot even credit Whitton with having originality," muttered Colin in a sarcastic tone. He was still smarting from the astonishing interchange with the headmistress of a school that was occupying what should have been the *empty* building he owned. Bergen had been right. He felt embarrassed for having blindly trusted the man's deed, especially after he had tried to kill him.

"One might assume," Morray began in a soft voice, "that Whitton's attempt to kill you transpired to conceal an illegality. We had assumed him to be bedeviled as a result of disappointing his family; however, it would appear he wanted to hide a more shameful act. Still, I am not inclined to think it planned. I see him more as an impulsive sort. And that fits his reputation. I do not think this was premeditated."

"I imagine the Countess will petition to see me, and before she does, I desire to have more facts before me. I suspect you are correct, Morray, and this deed may not be valid," agreed Colin, climbing into the carriage. His annoyance was rapidly turning into anger. "Mayhap I should try to be beforehand and call on her first."

Following closely behind Morray, Bergen snorted as he seated himself on the opposite bench.

"Her granddaughter is no shy miss. Rarely do you meet a woman who can deliver such a guileful blow without losing a hint of composure. Her grandmother would be proud, I think. The Countess is known to be quite charming and also a shrewd negotiator, so be warned."

"I hate to be a stickler, and I would be less inclined to cut up stiff had he not tried to kill me. Yet now, I find, I am more determined than ever that his debt be honored. This deed," he went on, patting the pocket holding the paper, "whether fake or real, should serve as a credible substitution for the debt he owes. My father was friends with the Countess' husband. He always considered the Earl an honest gentleman—a gentleman very different from his son."

"I have encountered Whitton in some of my dealings. I am afraid that his... ah... habits of late have driven the man towards some unscrupulous people. His level of desperation does not surprise me. What will surprise me is if the deed you hold is not a forgery. The headmistress sounded very certain of her advantage," Morray countered in an unaffected tone.

Colin smiled despite his wounded pride. "She was rather certain," he murmured, as his thoughts drifted back to their meeting. "At first, I thought she was inviting a negotiation over tea." He chuckled. "I will admit I did not expect such a worthy check." If he were honest, he mused, he had been rather engaged by her clever play. *If I were to marry, that would be the type of woman I would choose.*

"Ah… so you *noticed* the beautiful headmistress, Miss Mason," Bergen taunted, grinning.

"It is futile to bamboozle you, I see." Colin chuckled, feeling his irritation lifting. Bergen was always good to have about. "I believe I have just suffered checkmate at the hands of a lovely opponent," he agreed. *I noticed her.* No woman in memory had caused such inner conflict as this one had. An inconsequential touch over a teacup came to mind and he briefly wondered if it had affected her as it had him. Pulses of pleasure had raced up his arm. He felt more than a sense of annoyance. Surely, it was not attraction … *or was it?*

"I own that I cannot recall seeing her in any *ton* events, at least none that I can summon immediately to mind. There must be more to her story than meets the eye. She reminded me of my own Elizabeth," Bergen persisted, beaming. "She came with a menagerie of children and pets, and never ceases to make me merry!"

"Your wife is a genuine find," Colin agreed, lost in thought for a long moment before he finally continued, "I shall go to see the Countess tomorrow and make my case." Once she realizes that I am indeed owed this building, it will be resolved, he told himself.

"Since my family is residing with me in London at the moment, there is no reason whereby I cannot go with you tomorrow, should you so wish. I can bear witness to the events of that night," Bergen offered.

"A sound idea, Shefford. 'Tis a shame three might be a crowd." Morray spoke up. "I was just thinking about a loose end… and I hesitate to bring this up, yet have either of you enquired whether the Earl is still being held? I have heard that Sir Edward James, the magistrate, whom you mentioned leading Whitton away, held Lord Whitton's father in high regard. Based on the events of this day, I can imagine Whitton using that circumstance to his advantage."

"Of course! I mean, no; I have not checked, and you are right. I, too, recall seeing them in company together at White's before the older Earl passed away," Bergen said with an exaggerated exhale. "He might gain a measure of protection from his father's friends, who were not there to see him attempt to kill a peer."

"Our business is not without its perquisites. I shall consult with some of our connections, including the Earl of Baxter, and see what I may learn about our friend Whitton," Morray proposed sardonically. "I should look into his sister's family as well…"

"No, I should prefer to do that myself," Colin stated, noticing that both friends were smirking at him.

"What?" he demanded, feigning indignation.

"Do not even try to defend yourself, my friend." Morray laughed. "The lady definitely gained your notice."

The carriage turned off the road onto the small, semi-circular drive leading to Colin's house in Mayfair. It stopped in front of a three-story, grey stone mansion with a large, covered portico and tall windows rising from the first floor. A mixture of flowering evergreen shrubs lined the front of the walls, adding a sense of warmth to the home.

"I will take my leave, Shefford. Send a messenger when you decide what time we should meet with the Countess. I can meet you here and we may ride there together," Bergen said.

"I think I will head to the club. It might be well to let Baxter know what has happened these last few days. He may have information that could prove useful." Morray tipped his hat and went with Bergen towards the stables, located just behind the house.

Colin handed his greatcoat, hat, and cane to Franklin, intending to avail himself of brandy in his study and distract himself from thoughts of the vexing meeting with the lovely headmistress.

"You have had a visitor, my lord," the retainer said, holding out a silver salver on which lay a visiting card. "He was a short, balding individual with, if you will forgive my bluntness, a distasteful appearance and attitude. And Lady Shefford awaits your return in the drawing room."

"Thank you, Franklin." Colin barely glanced at the card before he stuffed it in his pocket and proceeded down the dimly lit hall to his office. *How odd. Franklin rarely remarks about visitors.* He was almost to his office when he recalled Franklin's last words. *His mother was here?* He wanted to look at that card again, but the sound of his mother's voice gained his attention.

"Davis, please bring my son and I some tea. I have no doubt he is hungry, so please have Cook add a small plate of meats and cheese."

"Yes, my lady. Right away."

Colin turned to see his mother approaching. The footman bowed and withdrew. He opened the door of the study and stood back for his mother to enter. "I was about to join you in the drawing room, ma'am."

"I thought you might need a little push, dearest, in case you became… distracted on your return," she said, walking to the fireplace and stretching her hands toward the welcoming warmth.

"By Jove, Mother—!" he protested. "That is outrageous."

"It is always nice to see this picture of your father," she mused, ignoring his outburst and looking up at the portrait over the mantel. "I recall that day well. It was the day after you went to Eton. He was so proud of you and could not wipe the smile from his face. If he said it once, he said it a dozen times, that he was glad you enjoyed attending his alma mater." She turned to him and wiped a single tear from the edge of her eye. "While we always valued your opinion, he had strong feelings about you attending the same school. When you wrote and told us how much you enjoyed it there, I could feel the pride emanating from him."

Colin looked at the portrait of his sire, who stood behind his mother, with her small dog, Pepper, seated in her lap. He had always admired this painting, for it portrayed his father in a more jovial mood than the traditional, unsmiling portraits. "I have not heard that story before, Mother." Neither had he realized the reason for the near smile on his patriarch's face until now.

"You resemble your father, Colin. He enjoyed the excitement life offered, yet he had a moral sense of duty." The Countess walked up to him and kissed him on the cheek. She looked as if she wanted to say more.

The footman chose that moment to return with the tea and refreshments.

"Place it on the side-table next to the leather chairs, Davis," Colin instructed, watching his mother move to the tea service.

"There! A small amount of sugar, just as you like it," she said as she handed the saucer of tea to him. It always seemed to taste better when his mother served the beverage, he thought, taking his first sip.

"I do have a reason for my visit," she said finally, taking her seat near him and setting her teacup down on the small table between the chairs. "I received a message yesterday that disturbed me. I read it several times and could not imagine its meaning. I believe whoever wrote it intended it for you, although that does not make me feel better."

"Your house is only a few doors from mine. I suppose it is conceivable someone could have mistaken the address and sent you a message intended for me. Did you bring it?" he queried as he swallowed a mouthful of meat and cheese and chased it with his tea. He was hungrier than he had imagined.

"Yes, I did," she responded softly. "I saw you leave this morning, just as I was about to bring it to you, so I waited a few hours before calling."

He cleared his throat and took another sip of tea. "Do you have it now?"

"I do." She reached into her pocket and withdrew a wrinkled paper.

Colin turned the paper over, curious as to why it was withered and dirty. There was a single message with no signature. Whitton!

Return the deed.

"This does concern me," he started slowly, noticing his mother staring at him as he once more glanced down at the message. *She already knows this is connected to me*, he thought. "Mother, I cannot imagine why you have received this." For a moment he debated what to tell her, deciding, in that instant, she could help him.

"I cannot conceive the why of it either," she returned. "Especially since they tied it to a brick and hurled it through my parlor window."

Colin fought the fury which mounted in his blood. The blighter must be deranged to throw a brick through his mother's parlor window, although it was possible the man could have confused the addresses. This was too much. It also seemed to affirm that he was not being held in gaol.

"Mother, it appears to be from Lord Whitton..."

"The man—I will not call him a gentleman—is a wastrel. I cannot imagine any business you might have with him," she said, cutting him off. "Seriously, though, Colin, you cannot but admit I have been most indulgent with your need for adventure. I have asked little of you and have waited patiently for you to *marry*." The last word was almost acerbic. "Pray tell me, what business have you entered with this man that he would do such a thing?"

"Mother, he wagered a deed for a building—that I had not until this morning even seen—on a game of chance. He lost." Colin decided it would be better to leave out the attempt on his life. His mother knew naught about his business dealings, and he wanted to keep it that way, as much as was possible. "I gave him the opportunity to pay his debt in full, even after losing the deed, and he has chosen this route instead. As it is, I am questioning the validity of the deed itself. It could be a forgery."

"Mercy! she exclaimed. "His family is of excellent stock. I cannot imagine what could have driven him to such lengths." She paused. "What more can you tell me about the circumstances of this... *debt?*"

He never doubted his mother's intelligence. She was astute. "It is supposed to be a vacant building in Russell Square. Morray, Bergen, and I went there this morning, to scrutinize it. It was not vacant. A Miss Mason has opened an orphanage there."

How strange. His mother smiled and suddenly, her demeanor changed.

"The Dowager Whitton's granddaughter?" she queried, yet it seemed she merely wished for confirmation.

"Do you know her? I do not recall ever seeing her at a *ton* event," he acknowledged, continuing ruminatively, "Miss Mason was most unwelcoming."

"Pish! She is a delightful young woman and most intelligent. I met her once at a tea party held by her grandmother. She came with her mother. A beautiful young woman, to be sure," she added, seeming to have forgotten the message wrapped around a brick and delivered through her glass window. "I did not have a chance to speak with her beyond the niceties."

He saw where this discourse was leading and struggled to put an end to it. He had no intention of becoming leg-shackled, even though Mother had effortlessly navigated onto her favorite topic—his marriage. Still, this information was useful.

"I will admit the young woman seems to be a diamond of the first water. That being said, I confess to being bemused as to why she has not had a come out," he probed gently. He would have remembered her, had they ever met. *Although she had begun to occupy his thoughts since their meeting.*

"Her mother disappointed *her* parents and eloped with a handsome young lieutenant... Peter, I believe is his name. It is a curious relationship. The Lady Eliza Mason, her mother, maintains a distance, socially. She visits her mother but has withdrawn from any activity which would require her to be with Society, including balls and entertainments. Her daughter is an unknown. Lady Mason's husband is the son of a barrister, who also was a merchant. I believe her husband also chose the law. I would have to determine the truth of that. However, the grandmother is very close to her granddaughter, a relationship encouraged by both parents. Because of the power of the Dowager Countess, her granddaughter has never been the subject of idle gossip. Neither has her mother, for that matter." Lady Shefford set down her saucer and directed a half smile in his direction.

"That answers a few questions, to be sure. Whitton has a reason to wish for the return of this deed, and I suspect it has something to do with an illegality. If what I suspect has occurred, it might not go well for him—even if his mother does not wish to pursue the matter."

"You infer that he may have falsified the deed," she stated matter-of-factly. "I would be careful of admitting that abroad, even though his reputation has never been savory." On those words, she stood up. "I am sure you will take care of this matter. Please extend my regards to both the Countess and her granddaughter, when you see them next."

"I will walk you home, Mother." He rushed to grab his coat and join her in the street, finding her change of attitude very odd. He kissed her cheek when they arrived at her residence and he glanced to the right of the entrance, at the broken pane of glass. Her staff had already covered it with a board. "I will take care of getting this repaired for you, Mother."

"Nonsense. I have already taken care of it," she said flatly as she reached her door.

He watched the door close behind her before turning and heading back to his own house. Needing to address a bothersome concern, he fished in his pocket and pulled out the card. As he walked into the light of his office, he read the scribbled name over one that had been scratched out.

Lord Wilford Montgomery, The Earl of Whitton

WHERE HE WAS MERELY CONCERNED before, he was now deeply troubled. Whitton apparently knew the house he had hurled a brick into belonged to Colin's mother, for this card had been left with Franklin. Morray's fears had been well-founded. The Earl had found his way out of the lock-up and was on his own business. *The question is... where is he hiding?* As he opened the door, he gained his butler's attention.

"Franklin, have my carriage brought back around, *immediately.*" The brandy he had imagined having an hour ago would have longer to wait.

CHAPTER 6

Finally, allowing herself to relax, Nora shut the door and leaned back against it, taking a fortifying gulp of air. She had known better than to show uncertainty, but since the gentlemen were now gone, many doubts accosted her. She squeezed her eyes shut, willing her body to become calm. What else could this morning bring her way? *What if the deed they hold is real?* She wished to believe it was a forgery, but knowing her uncle as she did, she could not take the chance.

The cook scurried from the parlor, carrying a tray of cups, saucers, and the empty teapot.

"Mrs. Simpkins," Nora called softly, hoping not to perturb the woman and cause her to drop the china. The woman was forever moving in rapid motion.

The housekeeper slowed and turned. "Ah, there ye are, Miss Nora! I had wondered where ye had gone. How did it go with the gentlemen?"

"Well, and not so well, if that makes any sense. The tea helped, and your lemon biscuits were, of course, delicious. However, Lord Shefford holds a deed for this property, signed by my uncle."

"That cannae be right. Lady Whitton would ne'er do such a thing,"

Mrs. Simpkins responded. "Ye need to speak with yer grandmama afore ye get in a pucker," she cautioned.

"I have the same thought in mind. I should go to her… but will you be able to manage matters here without me?"

"Aye, I can, that. Never doubt it, lass." Her gaze swung past Nora to the narrow window beside the door. "Will ye ever believe it? If the Countess hasnae just rolled up in her fancy chariot!"

"Really?" Nora looked out of the window. Waving her walking cane in emphasis, Grandmama was instructing a footman in her requirements. Then she turned and walked up the steps. "Good gracious, she is here!" All at once, a rush of anticipation and dread filled her. She repressed her anxiety and fixed her attention instead on the man accompanying her grandmother. *Who is he? I need no more shocks this day.* Nora took a calming breath and opened the door.

"Grandmama! What a pleasant and welcome surprise!"

"Nora, is something wrong? I thought we had agreed I should visit today," the Countess asked, concern evident in her voice.

"Yes, yes, of course! You are quite correct. Forgive me; I am at sixes and sevens. Come in and warm yourself. There is a pleasant fire in the parlor. Mrs. Simpkins is fetching some tea and lemon biscuits." It was perfect timing, but how had she forgotten her grandmother was to visit today? *Disordered nerves!* Nora took a deep, steadying breath.

"That sounds like a lovely idea. I have some matters I wish to discuss with you, and afterwards, I would like to see what you have done here," her grandmother replied.

"I am a little done up, although otherwise quite well, Grandmama.

"Before we go further, allow me to introduce you to one of my most trusted menservants."

Nora opened the door and a lackey came in carrying a trunk. She looked back to the curb and saw two more trunks and a large, handled wooden box.

"I have brought Amos Woods to help you with whatever you need doing, whether inside or outside the house. He will serve the duties of footman and watchman. I would feel better if you would direct him to answer the door when you do not have any other duties for him." She turned to the servant. "This is my granddaughter, Miss Honoria Mason. She is the headmistress here, and I wish you to do whatever you can to make easier the lives of the children and women living here. Place the trunks in the parlor, if you please, and remove them to where Miss Mason desires, when I leave. I have some items for Nora and the children."

"Yes, my lady," he answered before returning for the rest.

Nora realized that her mouth was hanging open in a foolish fashion and swiftly closed it.

"Thank you, Grandmama. That is so thoughtful of you. We shall be glad of the help. Will he take the place of ... ?"

"The gardener?" her grandmother finished for her.

Nora nodded.

"No, my dear. Marsh will continue helping with your garden and assist you with maintenance." She nodded towards Amos Woods. "Woods also has certain skills as a handyman and given your desire to open as much of the building as possible, as soon as may be, I thought the additional labor would be beneficial."

Mrs. Simpkins entered then, interrupting their conversation, and gave a small curtsey before setting down a tea tray.

"Would ye like for me to pour?" she asked.

"Thank you, Mrs. Simpkins, we will makeshift for ourselves. Would you be so kind as to show Mr. Amos Woods, our new footman, handyman, and man of all work to a bedchamber?" Nora asked, putting forth a cheeriness in her voice she did not feel. She noticed her grandmother observing her.

"Yes, miss. I will be happy to," the retainer responded, before withdrawing from the room.

"Shall we have tea, my dear? I must say that I have missed Mrs. Simpkins's lemon biscuits."

Nora found herself grinning, as she watched Mr. Woods deliver the final trunk. Her grandmother's visits were a welcomed respite from the rest of her day. She would never be too old for Grandmama's surprises.

The Countess finished her tea and looked with satisfaction at the stack of trunks. "Come, now. I would like to see what you have accomplished. It would bring me immense pleasure to meet these children," Lady Whitton prompted. "We will get to those later." She gave a short wave towards the boxes and trunks in the corner of the room.

Brightening, Nora thought immediately of little Amy and her devoted friend, Alice. "You must meet the two newest children, Grandmama. They are not sisters, but they are as sweet together as any two children could be. Little Amy's mother died of a dread disease caused by her occupation. We have a wonderful group of children." She glanced up at the wooden clock on the fireplace mantelshelf. I believe they will be washing their hands for their midday meal. Nonetheless, I would love you to see their rooms."

"That would be delightful. Shall we, my dear?" the Countess said. She rose from her chair and extended her arm to her granddaughter. "We will chat afterward."

Nora took her grandmother's arm and led her up the stairs and down the hall to the children's large room, where they found the children in two lines, washing their faces and hands at the two bowls set upon a large table, one or two of the older children helping the little ones.

"The room is very tidy, even with such a large number of children, and they are so well-behaved," Grandmama observed in excited tones. "I am delighted you chose to begin our tour here. The room is so cheery, and that is good for the children."

Nora cleared her throat and clapped her hands. "Children, we have an esteemed visitor today, who I would like you to meet. This is the Countess of Whitton. It is because of her generosity that we have this wonderful school."

At her announcement, a dark-haired boy of about eight, and a tow-headed stripling a year or two older, attempted to bow politely. Grandmama smiled her pleasure. Not to be outdone, a red-headed girl and an eight-year-old girl came forward and curtseyed. The others cheered, with two exceptions…

Before she could ask, a small child of six emerged from behind the bigger children, holding the hand of a toddler. "Grandmama, these are the two girls I wished to introduce you to," whispered Nora, watching them walk towards them. Amy threw her arms up when she came near enough; leaning down, Nora picked her up.

"This is Amy, and this is Alice. I mentioned them a few minutes ago, if you recall," Nora said softly. "Amy arrived two days ago and Alice came a day or two after we opened." Affectionately, she smoothed the older child's blonde curls. "Alice has already become a wonderful big sister to Amy."

The Countess lowered herself until she was level with Alice. "Young lady, I have some special gifts for everyone. The only question that remains for me to ask is what are your favorite colors?" She gave a small nod to Alice.

"I once had a doll with a pink dress. Pink is my favorite color," the little girl answered happily. "And Amy likes it, too," she finished.

Nora crouched down with Amy, wanting to be part of this small gathering.

"Indeed!" Grandmama looked at the smallest girl. "Do you like pink?" she asked merrily. Amy's red curls bounced up and down in affirmation, and Nora was pleased to see a smile forming on her lips. "Then, perhaps I selected the right surprises," she said cheerily.

"It is a delight to meet you both," the Countess said, giving each a small hug, before standing up again. She turned to Nora. "We have a few things to discuss, so we should continue our tour."

Nora put Amy down and showed her grandmother around the living rooms and the classrooms, pointing out what her plans were in the unfinished areas. She needed paint, some carpentry, and cabinetry and was thrilled by the addition of Amos Woods as a man of all work. With his labor and that of the gardener, Marsh, she envisioned living in more comfortable circumstances. She planned to teach the fundamentals of reading, writing, arithmetic, and manners. In addition, she intended to provide some essential skills which would eventually enable the children to secure safe employment, away from the streets and the life they would, most likely, have faced without her intervention.

41

"I can see that your present situation agrees with you, Nora," her grandmother said, shaking her from her reverie.

"Yes, Grandmama, I believe it does. I enjoy having the opportunity to help these children, and being able to contribute, in a positive way, to society. I wish for them to learn a trade so they might better themselves and have skills to rely upon in times of uncertainty." Her own family situation was a salutary reminder of that necessity, she thought ruefully.

Once the door to the parlor had closed behind them, the Countess stepped forward and gave her granddaughter a big hug.

"Tell me, child, what is the matter?"

"You *know*?" Nora's vision misted.

"I *see* you are troubled, girl, and that is all I need to understand." She gently wiped the tears from Nora's eyes and looked around the room.

"I am worried about the future of the orphanage, Grandmama," Nora admitted as calmly as she could.

"Nonsense. You have accomplished much here, my dear. What has you so upset?"

Nora sought to avoid regaling her grandmother with the details of Lord Shefford's call. She wished this visit could be only about the children and thus had preferred to show her the orphans' adorable faces—faces belonging to the children Grandmama had helped. Nonetheless, Nora needed to know the truth. She drew in a sharp breath. "Grandmama, I had a visitor earlier this morning—three visitors, in fact. They left shortly before you arrived. The Lords Shefford, Bergen, and Morray called on me. Lord Shefford had in his possession a deed to this building which Uncle Wilford had signed." She searched her grandmother's face, and the disbelief she saw in that lady's expression acknowledged her worst fears.

"Lud! My son has *sold* the building?" the Countess exclaimed, her face coloring red. "How can that be?"

The response was *not* what Nora had hoped to hear. She grappled with the icy feeling of shock and fear in the pit of her stomach.

"Grandmama, Uncle did not sell it. He *lost* it… at the card table."

Her grandmother opened her mouth to speak, but then closed it and stayed quiet for a moment.

"I will look into this immediately. In the meantime, I do not wish for you to worry about your orphanage, Nora. Come, let us be seated." They both moved to the sofa. "This is highly improbable, my dear. My husband, your grandpapa, gave me this property, and I have kept it separate from the estate business." She patted Nora's hand. "I will resolve this. I should speak with Lord Shefford. If your uncle has hoodwinked a peer, there could be a steep price to pay, and I will be the least of his worries. Shefford is a powerful gentleman, and while I am not without my own connections, this could be disastrous for your uncle."

"I shall do my best not to worry, then." Nora spoke the words although she did not feel the sentiment. *Where will my children go? Who will care for them if there is no orphanage?*

CHAPTER 7

A few hours after taking his leave of Miss Mason, Colin directed his carriage to stop and he and Bergen took the steps to the club two at a time. Anxiety was palpable in his friend's demeanor—and no doubt his own—as Colin pulled on the brass lion bell.

A tall man with greying hair answered the door. "Lord Shefford, Lord Bergen, good evening. How may I be of help?"

"Henry, has Lord Morray arrived?" Colin inquired.

"He is here, my lord. I believe he went to Lord Baxter's office."

"Excellent." Morray had undoubtedly already spoken to Baxter. "Thank you," Colin returned, as he and Bergen handed their coats and hats to the doorman.

"I was here earlier and heard Baxter moved his office to the second floor. We can access it with the back stairs," Bergen supplied as the two men hurried down the hall. They pulled the door open to the hallway and knocked on the ornate wooden door in front of them. Hearing an invitation, they entered.

"I am glad to find you both here," Colin said without preamble. "I need your help." He looked at Morray. "You were right. Whitton persuaded the magistrate to release him and he has threatened my family—my mother, to be specific."

"What happened?" Morray withdrew his cigar from his mouth and pressed it out in the ashtray sitting next to him.

"This situation with Whitton has grown out of control. I cannot conjecture why the magistrate has let him go. However, the man threw a stone through the window of my mother's townhouse and followed that infamous act by leaving a card at mine," Shefford stated, much more calmly than he felt. "I will not allow the man to threaten my family."

"Was a note attached to the stone?" Morray asked.

"Yes. It told her to return the deed. Of course, Mother would not know to what he was referring."

"Give me a few hours to find him," Baxter offered. "We have connections, and avenues not open to the majority of Society."

"We will find Whitton," Morray added. "The man needs to be brought to justice."

"Morray has acquainted me with the facts. However, there is more I would like to know before I petition lords and magistrates. Take a seat and join us. I have just ordered a light repast. There should be plenty for the four of us." Baxter pulled a cord beside the fireplace. "It will give me a chance to hear more about the game which could have done for two of my best men."

"Your mother, is she unharmed?" Morray inquired.

"She is." He nodded his thanks. "Thankfully, she did not feel threatened either. Of course, it was one more opportunity to see her matchmaking schemes in motion. As soon as I mentioned Miss Honoria Mason's name, I could practically see the wheels turning."

"Do be careful! Matchmaking mamas can be fierce when they think they are being deprived of grandbabies." Baxter guffawed.

"We cannot all be so fortunate as to find a wonderful bride such as you have found with Lady Baxter," Colin acknowledged with a grin.

"She is a treasure," Baxter returned, smiling from ear to ear. "She has added an element to my life I never before realized was missing."

"Still, I plan to delay that step for a goodly while yet," returned Colin.

"Yes, so have we all said," chuckled Baxter. "We should return to the business at hand."

"The man is dangerous. I am not completely sure he has not run mad!" remarked Bergen. "He came at us from the dark, completely unexpected. Had it not been for our instincts and the boy we had hired to watch the horses, he could, at the least, have seriously injured Shefford."

"One can never underestimate a deranged man," Morray agreed as he passed a ledger to Shefford. "I paid a visit on a contact whilst on my way to the club. He has just delivered this to me. Look."

"Whew!" Colin exhaled slowly. "I almost feel sorry for him," he muttered, turning the pages of the ledger. "He has taken out loans which are now due. Are his properties not prosperous?"

"His father's wealth was known well. However, the son has not capably managed it. In the few years since his sire's death, he has, it appears, lost quite a tidy sum. The elder lord expected it. In a highly controversial move, the Dowager Countess maintains control of much of the wealth, as unusual as that may seem. Her husband trusted her business acumen enough that, before his death, he passed much of the ready coin and most important property deeds into her control. I must admit, she has made wise investments through her husband's former man of business. The banks respect her."

"I see a couple of notations on one or two deeds, but not the deed to the building I am supposed to now own." For a moment, Colin felt better about the bargain. "I hope..."

"That the property in question was in his possession," finished Baxter in a wry voice. "Perhaps. My parents used to remark about the charitable contributions the older Whitton made to support an orphanage and school which occupied that building some years ago. Lady Whitton worked there when the Earl met her. It would not surprise me if they separated it."

Baxter's words settled upon him, and Colin felt his shoulders slump. "You are inferring the opposite of what I need to believe. You think she may hold that deed, herself." In that moment, he tried to imagine what he would say to Jonathan. Thinking the only thing he needed to do was survey the property, he had sent word to Jonathan, almost promising his brother they had the site for the fencing club.

Baxter gave a quick nod in Bergen's direction. "Morray told me of the fencing club you and your brother wish to build. It holds appeal for me, as well. I would be a willing investor."

"It was Jonathan's idea and he will run it. We aspire to honor our father, who was a considerable proponent of fencing. Father encouraged all of us to learn. Although the popularity is not what it once was, the skills can make the difference in life and death." Colin was rarely without his cane, which concealed a rapier inside. It had been a gift from his father. Ironically, he had not taken it with him on the night Whitton stabbed him. That mistake only reinforced his desire to open the fencing club. "At least this gives me a better idea of my position when I meet with the Countess."

Morray coughed. "It is a ticklish position. Has she asked to see you?" Morray inquired. "We passed her carriage when we left the school. I assumed she was going to see her granddaughter."

"Yes. I expect she will send for me. However, I am not sure I can wait. I plan to call upon her when I leave here," Colin responded.

A knock sounded on the door before it opened and a footman entered, carrying a tray of meats and cheeses.

"Lord Morray, I have a message for you," the footman said, after setting the tray on a side-table.

"Thank you, Jeffers," Morray returned, accepting the note and reading it.

The footman bowed and left the room.

"Gentlemen, please do not be shy. Help yourselves to a light meal. We have tea, or can offer something stronger, should you prefer," Baxter said.

"Tea will do for me," Morray responded, tucking the note into his pocket.

"I will take tea as well," Colin added.

Bergen had already poured himself a glass of brandy from the open liquor cabinet.

Colin realized he was hungry. Helping themselves, the four men ate for a few minutes in silence, enjoying the variety of foods in front of them. As he munched on a small selection of meats and cheeses, he thought about what lay ahead of him. He wished circumstances did not dictate a meeting with the Countess, but it could not be avoided. She was reputed to be both witty and sharp, and a decent negotiator. While he feared no meeting, a plaguy feeling told him this was one occasion when he should.

"The note Jeffers delivered is from one of my contacts. Whitton is hiding in his ladybird's apartment on Baker Street. The woman's name is Jenny Maven."

Morray's words broke through his thoughts.

"She works at the gaming hell where all of this started," Bergen added. "The woman served drinks and also ruffled his hair while he was playing." He chuckled. "I found the exchange entertaining."

"Now that you mention it, I recall a woman doing that. Did she not have dark hair and blue eyes, and was rather plump? It seems like she wore some sort of feathered headdress, now that I think about it." Colin added.

"The very one. My, what close notice you took," Bergen offered a wry smile. "She also employed an overly seductive walk when she left the table. Whitton acknowledged her by name."

"That makes it easier to find him. I want him back under lock and key. The brick which broke my mother's front window was no accident." Colin said.

"You mentioned that vexation," Baxter remarked. "We wish for him to account for his crime when they arrest him. I might suggest we send a couple of Runners to apprehend him."

"I can take care of that, and I have just the place to keep him." Morray smirked. "I will also send word to the Prince Regent on Whitton's activities. He is not held in the highest esteem, judging from the way no one raised so much as an eyebrow when the previous Earl moved much of his wealth to his wife's control. Whitton appealed the changes, but perhaps, because of a lengthy letter from his father, included with a copy of the Will, nothing changed."

"I do not believe the Regent would even consider changing a Will, letter or no letter," added Baxter. "Let his mother know about his activities and she may take care of the situation herself," he suggested, wiping his hands on the napkins provided with the meal.

"I appreciate everyone's efforts on my behalf." Colin flicked at an imaginary piece of lint from the leg of his breeches and then stood up. "I have one more call to make today, and I need to make the most of the afternoon. I should not put it off any longer or I will be cursing myself by evening for procrastinating."

"Say 'Good afternoon' to the Countess." Morray snorted at his own jest.

"You will find her a worthy opponent. Stay sharp," Baxter warned as he, too, stood up.

When he and Bergen left the club, Colin had the overwhelming feeling that life as he knew it was about to change yet could not determine why he felt that way. *It is a woman, for goodness' sake.*

Bergen and he rode quietly towards Mayfair. The Countess' house was one of the largest and grandest in the area. Colin considered how Whitton must have felt when his father withdrew Whitton's control from most of their family's funds and gave power to his mother instead. That could test a man's ability to keep his head. Colin did not, however, have too much time to reflect. His carriage halted only a moment before a pair of black iron gates opened and then closed behind them as they approached the four-storied stone house.

The door opened as soon as he and Bergen stepped from the carriage. "Good afternoon, Lord Shefford, Lord Bergen," a tall, thin man, with thick grey hair and dark brown eyes, greeted them when they mounted the steps. He waved them towards a grand stairwell. "The Countess is expecting you. Please follow me."

Clearly, the woman had him at a disadvantage, Colin mused. *How did she know I would call upon her?* A warm feeling shot up his neck.

Stepping onto the landing, the retainer led him directly across the hall to closed double-doors. Before he had another moment to think about it, the man opened the door to a spacious drawing room. "The Lords Shefford and Bergen, your ladyship," the retainer said.

Bergen and Colin crossed into a room tastefully decorated in pale gold, creamy whites, and burgundy. A large, burgundy Axminster carpet interwoven with subtle patterns of cream covered the floor, while a patterned cream damask wallpaper and a matching large sofa brought their attention to the center of the room. The room was separated by the settee into two sections. Behind the sofa, a large mahogany pianoforte graced the front of large windows covered with burgundy velvet drapes, held back on each side with gold-colored tasseled ropes. A bouquet of red roses filled the room with scent from a round, marbled table sitting to the right of the settee.

"Thank you, Masters. Please have some refreshments sent up."

"Yes, my lady." The retainer bowed and left.

"Good afternoon, my lady." Simultaneously, Colin and Bergen effected a bow displaying an elegant leg.

The grey-haired, buxom Countess sat down on her cream and gold settee, smoothing the skirt of her deep blue satin dress, she encouraged both men to be seated. They each took a burgundy-covered mahogany armchair facing the couch.

"Gentlemen, I fear we should get straight to the point," the Countess stated in a matter-of-fact tone. "I have just left my grand-daughter, Nora, and my orphanage. She is most unhappy."

Shefford shifted subtly in his seat, and glanced at his friend, who hastily tried to hide the surprise on his face. "You come straight to the point, my lady," Shefford said, withdrawing a folded parchment from his waistcoat. "I will do so as well." He rose and walked over to her, handing her the deed.

"Is this the deed you showed to my granddaughter?"

"It is, Countess." Remaining detached, Colin watched her scrutinize the document. She then picked up a small leather pouch and withdrew an envelope. Picking up the envelope, she held it close to her as she spoke.

"Many years ago, my husband gave me a gift. He did so from senti-mentality, but it meant a great deal to me. When Nora told me of your visit, for a moment I wondered if my son had somehow secured my gift for his own nefarious ends." She passed him her small packet.

He opened the envelope, feeling a mixture of dread, anger, and frustration. Reading the parchment clarified that his deed was a forgery. However, the fact her son had forged a deed and used it to pay a debt still gave him a measure of influence, at least in his mind. He looked up.

"What do you suggest? Obviously, you have a legitimate deed and I have a forgery." He paused, debating how to gain the advantage. "I am not sure how much of your son's behavior you are aware of."

"I know that my son is a prolific gambler and womanizer. My husband tried very hard to reform him, to no avail. I can think of naught we did not try." She took a deep breath. "You will probably be unaware of this, but my husband moved everything unentailed to my care before he died. I still owe my husband inordinate gratitude for allowing us to preserve our holdings this way. It has only added to my son's anger and resentment. Yet I consider that a small price compared with the very real likelihood we would have lost our home, given his flagrant need to drink and gamble."

"I have heard you have made some astute investments."

"Is that what they say?" She laughed sarcastically.

"My lady, how do you propose that we resolve this problem?" Colin asked, feeling very frustrated, as the Countess passed the forged document back to him. "I am still owed the blunt."

"Would you mind sharing with me the amount you are owed and how the bet transpired?" she asked.

Colin recounted the information. By his calculations, he had been owed a little over a thousand pounds and had accepted the deed as payment. Bergen could verify that if it proved necessary.

"If I am to understand this correctly, you accepted this *deed*, without accounting for its worth?" She drew herself up straighter.

Colin felt himself cringe. How had he not anticipated this?

"My lord, surely you realize *your deed is worthless*." Her eyes met his.

"I prefer to think of it as his vowels, my lady," Colin returned. He sounded more confident than he felt.

"Countess, there is another important matter I would bring to your attention," Bergen put in. Without waiting for her answer, he continued, "Your son attempted to kill Lord Shefford. He attacked him with a knife as we left the gaming hall."

Colin noticed that she did not lose her composure. Why did he have the feeling she already knew of Whitton's infamy?

"That does make a difference," she conceded and was quiet for a moment. "I have a proposal for you."

He hoped she would honor her son's debt.

"First, I wish for your word... both of your words... that this conversation will not be repeated," she said slowly.

"You have my word," Colin responded.

Bergen nodded his assent.

"This orphanage is important to me, and I wish for it to have at least the chance of survival. My granddaughter does not understand that your deed is a fake. I would like you to make an agreement with her. She needs to realize how accomplished she is. Give her two weeks to prove to you that the orphanage is more worthwhile than any use you may otherwise have for it. I expect you will require to spend considerable time there, or else your proposition will not appear authentic. In the meantime, I will tell her I am investigating the deed. That would normally take time. I will continue to support her. Nora, like her parents and, indeed, myself..." She smiled pleasantly. "...has a great deal of pride and will not mention this arrangement, I am certain."

"I am flummoxed, my lady. How does this benefit me?" Colin tried to suppress his irritation yet was aware of a sharp note in his voice.

"I would like your appraisal of how my granddaughter does when forced to weigh her needs against the needs of others—as with the school, which already has fourteen children relying upon her." She smiled. "There are certain intentions... certain aims I have for her which I would like to see fulfilled."

"Ma'am, I think I should tell you I am far from happy with my role in this," he said, no longer able to hide his annoyance.

"Indulge me in this matter and you will have the choice of that building or, should you decide the orphanage is worthwhile, as I hope, I will give you the value of the property instead, which is considerable, and you may purchase another suitable for your purpose." She was quiet for a moment. "As for my son's attempt on your life—I only ask that you show some mercy. I love my son, but I cannot get him to see the error of his ways. I do not wish him hurt, of course, but he should answer for his actions."

Colin felt his mouth hang open and quickly closed it.

"Lord Shefford, are we in agreement?" she said, rising from her chair.

Standing up at once, Colin looked first to Bergen and then back at Lady Whitton. To all appearances, the arrangement seemed harmless, an exercise in futility. And he would spend time with the incomparable Miss Honoria Mason. What were the objections? *I have never made a more certain bet.*

Bergen stood following Colin. He cleared his throat and idly, seemed to unfasten and refasten a button on his waistcoat.

"My lady, I can see no harm in your proposal. Two weeks does not seem an interminable amount of time for me to wait before beginning my own project. I accept your terms."

Colin glanced at Bergen and noticed his friend's strained expression. This agreement was stacked in his favor. What could possibly have Bergen at sixes and sevens?

He and Bergen bowed. Having given his answer, Colin suddenly felt eager to leave. This whole meeting felt surreal to him.

Five minutes later, he and Bergen walked down the steps of the townhouse and into the carriage.

When the door to the carriage closed, Bergen turned to Shefford. "There is more to this than meets the eye. You realize that do you not?"

"I allow her granddaughter to continue to indulge her charitable inclinations with this orphanage project and she honors her son's debt to me. I may stand to make a profit. It is simple enough." He adjusted his hat and relaxed against the black leather squabs of his carriage.

"*That* is what you heard?" Bergen persisted.

"It is…" Colin stopped and considered his friend. "I will spend two weeks with her granddaughter—her very attractive, unmarried granddaughter—" He broke off again as the ghastly truth hit him. *By God,* he had just been bamboozled!

CHAPTER 8

*N*ora woke to the sound of a child softly whimpering and another one whispering. She slowly opened her eyes and saw Alice standing next to her bed, holding Amy's hand. Amy had tears streaming down her thin cheeks and wet auburn curls stuck to the sides of her face.

"Amy misses her mam," the older child explained, pulling Amy to her. "She was crying, so I climbed into the crib and Becca helped me get her out so's I could bring her to you."

"Oh, gracious! That was very thoughtful of the two of you. Did you notice where Becca went?" Nora asked thoughtfully. It concerned her that the other child might wander about the house. There were too many sections still under construction and the child could be injured.

"Becca crawled back into bed. Didn't take long fer her to go to sleep. I know, 'cause she snores. Her cot's next t' mine."

Nora smiled. "You were right to bring Amy to me," she said, meaning it. Her curtains were open to the full moon, allowing the brightness to filter into the room and give her plenty of light to see the two girls. She had always preferred moonlight to having a pitch-black room. "Hmm, I am not sure what time it is, but the moon is still out and 'tis very dark." She sidled across the mattress, against the wall, thus making room for the two girls, and patted the space next to her. "Climb up here, both of you. We will not make a habit of this, mind you, but just this once, it can do no harm."

The two girls crawled up into her bed and snuggled under the warm covers, with Amy nudging herself tightly against Nora's chest. Nora lay for several minutes, listening to the soft snores of the two children. A strange yearning tugged at her heart, one she had never felt before. She looked at the angelic faces of both girls and realized a desire to have children of her own, one day. Unfortunately, with no prospects, Nora felt she was destined to be a spinster, a future that, until this very moment, she had not minded. Determined to sleep, she squeezed her eyes closed, only to feel a lone tear escape and roll across the bridge of her nose before falling to her pillow.

The night passed without further incident. When Nora awoke the next morning and stretched her arms, movement to her left riveted her attention on the two little girls. They were sitting together in a worn green tapestry-covered chair, quietly drinking milk and eating a biscuit each.

"You really did come in here last night, then, my dears." She swallowed a giggle. "I wondered if I had dreamed the whole thing." She swung across to the side of the bed and slipped her feet inside the warm slippers that she kept nearby and looked at the younger little girl. "Do you feel well now, Amy?"

"She does," answered Alice. "She told me so."

"I have never heard her speak more than a word or two," Nora teased. "What did she say?" Nora had noticed that Alice had become so protective of Amy that she kept the toddler close to her and even spoke for her. The small child did not seem to object and stayed quiet.

"Amy said she was glad you let us sleep with you," Alice answered brightly.

Nora chuckled. "I am surprised Mrs. Simpkins did not take you back to your beds," she remarked hopefully. She knew Mrs. Simpkins had a soft heart where children were concerned, which made Nora doubly glad of the cook's help with the orphanage.

"She asked if we wanted to go to our room or wait until she came back with your chocolate. We stayed here," Alice offered, licking her fingers.

"You are lucky indeed, not to have been frog-marched back to your rooms," she smiled, glad they had chosen to stay. "And young ladies do not lick their fingers," Nora reproved, not desiring to scold, but needing to use the moment to educate. Alice immediately dried her fingers on the hem of her dress and sat up straighter. Amy stayed intent on the biscuit she was nibbling and took no heed.

"Amy cried so bad, I didn't know what to do. Becca woke up and helped me get her out. She likes you, so we found your room," Alice explained in between bites of the shortbread biscuit. "Becca went back to bed. She said we'd both get a whipping for waking you, but I didn't think you was mean like that," Alice continued.

"A whipping?" The idea alarmed Nora. She tried to recall where Becca had come from. Had they whipped the child? She supposed that many of the children had not been treated kindly before they arrived at the orphanage and made a mental note to pay more attention to Becca.

"'Tis time you both return to your room. I must dress." The children nodded. Standing, she pulled her wrapper from the chest at the end of her bed. Drawing the silk about her, she glanced out of the window. "We look to have a lovely day ahead of us, girls, and you will miss breakfast if you stay here much longer." Nora heard the rumbling in her own stomach and determined they could all use a good meal. "Hurry now, my dears! It is hardly seemly for a head-mistress to break her fast, thus scantily dressed, you know. Mrs. Simpkins will ring the bell for breakfast shortly, I am sure. We should not be late." Nora picked up Amy and walked the two girls downstairs to the communal dining room. The men had finally finished working on it. The rooms were slowly taking shape, she reflected.

On her way back to her bedchamber a little later, she met Mrs. Simpkins by the stairs.

"I noticed you had company last night," the cook said, smiling. "Those two girls are attached to you."

"I know—as I am to them," Nora said out loud, realizing how true it was. "Once they learn they can climb out..."

"They do it over and over," laughed Mrs. Simpkins. "'I will look for another bed in the attic. I was up there yesterday and found a box of broadcloth I think we can use, if we wash it. The mice did not do too much damage."

Nora winced. She would never get used to the mice. Her parents' home, while not grand, rarely had the little creatures. "I am hoping we can drive those pesky things out of here. I should speak to Grandmama about perhaps installing a couple of cats."

"I didn't see any evidence of rats, which is unusual, considering how long the building was empty," Mrs. Simpkins added. "If we adopt some cats, I would be 'appy to take care of them. I like the dear creatures."

"I plan to visit with Grandmama later this morning and will ask her thoughts on the matter. Will you ladies be able to take charge without me for a few hours?" Nora wanted to gain an idea of how long it might take to learn about Lord Shefford's supposed deed to this building. She felt reluctant to add any more mouths to their care, even cats, if it meant an obnoxious lord who cared only about his winnings, would soon displace them.

"Aye, Miss Mason. I believe we can come up trumps." The older woman winked.

While Nora realized her thinking was unkind, she did not relish another meeting with *his lordship*. Jaded by both her mother's and her own experiences with Society, she maintained what she called *a civil distance* from the *ton*. She loved her grandmother dearly, yet she could not but suspect that dear lady of machinations whereby she might endeavor to introduce Nora into Polite Society.

Her mother had felt the sting of the *ton's* dismissal when she married a soldier who was also the son of a well-established merchant. instead of a man of her own rank. When her grandfather's business failed, Society turned its back completely and the few contracts Grandpapa had thought he could count on were withdrawn, sending him into bankruptcy. By association, Grandpapa's fall from grace had destroyed her own father's fortunes. With the barest number of servants, her father had strived to keep a roof over the heads of her two brothers, her sister and herself, being unwilling to ask anything of his in-laws.

As a young girl, Nora had vowed she would not add to her parents' misery by sharing their misfortune with Grandmama, although she suspected her grandparents had both known. *Uncle knew.* He had lorded over them with his veiled threats, like the one to sell this building.

Shaking off her musing, Nora finished her ablutions. Not having had a lady's maid of her own, she had become proficient at getting in and out of her clothing, despite the difficulty her undergarments presented. The seamstress had helped by championing buttons and a dress style designed to open down the front. Deciding to wear her yellow and white striped muslin, with a yellow sash and her sensible half-boots, she quickly dressed.

Securing her braided hair into a low chignon, she dabbed at the edges of the tightly confined locks and pulled a few small curls forward. She thought of Becca's comments about whipping and, reminding herself of her intention to befriend the child, laid down her brush. If she hurried, she could catch the children before they finished breakfast.

She also felt an overwhelming need to see little Amy and make sure she and Alice were well. Nora could not imagine what went through the children's minds. Bridging the void left by the loss of parents remained an insurmountable task. She peeped into the room where the children were sitting and eating at long wooden tables with bench seats. Amy and Alice were eating together. Everyone seemed well enough, although she did not see Becca.

"Miss Mason, this note came for you." Mary's voice sounded from behind her and pulled her from her thoughts. "I believe it was from that woman who brought little Amy to us."

"'Aunt' Gemma? Did she ask to see Amy?"

"No, ma'am. Quite the opposite. She insisted that I not disturb either you or little Amy. She only wanted her note delivered." Mary looked down at her clasped hands before adding, "Ma'am, Miss Gemma had a lot of bruising on her face and looked ill."

A sick feeling clenched Nora's stomach. She knew of the atrocities that were committed in the East End, where Aunt Gemma lived, and praised her lucky stars that the woman had brought Amy to them as she sat down to read the handwritten note.

Miss Mason,

Please do not let little Amy out of your sight. A man named Mr. Sneed claims she is his, but she ain't. And he got naught to prove it. Amy's mother was my best friend and asked me to keep her baby safe. She told me she did not know who the father was. By my thinking, that means Mr. Sneed can't know, either. I believe with my heart he would raise Amy to steal. That ain't no life for her. Her mam wanted better. Tell our baby I love her.

Aunt Gemma

SNEED? Nora had never heard the surname before. If Gemma was right, the man meant to train Amy for the streets. Nora vowed never to allow that to happen. Meeting Grandmama would have to wait. Nora needed to ensure no one would harm Amy. She darted down to the hall and called Mrs. Simpkins and Mary.

"Miss Mason, is there something wrong? Was it the note?" Mary was out of breath, hurrying downstairs from the children's room, where she was no doubt tidying up and helping with the younger children.

"Yes, the note concerns me," Nora acknowledged. "I have questions I must ask of you. Did Aunt Gemma say anything else? Think hard, please, because it could be important."

Mary bit her lip and cast her eyes down, as if struggling to recall.

"Is something wrong, Miss Mason?" Mrs. Simpkins hastened into the front hall, a little winded from rushing from the kitchen, wiping her hands on her apron.

"I have received a disturbing note." Nora pulled it from her pocket and passed it to Mrs. Simpkins, whose eyes only grew larger as she read it.

"It speaks of a man who is passing himself off as Amy's father. We all know that there was no father. Had there been a responsible sire for the child, her mother may not have died in the way she did." Nora stopped. Her explanation sounded most uncharitable, and she had not meant to slander the poor woman. "I did not mean that as harsh as it sounded," she amended. "It is most important that, should anyone inquire about the child while I am gone, you do not give any affirmation that she is here. Amy's own mother did not know of a father for her child, and this man... this creature... is probably gathering small children to teach them to steal or send up the chimneys. From what I know, it is a horrible business and they treat children like animals." Tears sprang to her eyes. "Keep them inside until I return. I do not want our dear children to end up like that. Do not allow this man entry." She then turned to her cook. "Mrs. Simpkins, do you know where Woods might be working? I would like him to be on duty at the door, in case I have need of him."

"No, ma'am. After his meal, I noticed him returning upstairs to work on some of the rooms that needed maintenance. I think he is working on the boy's bedchambers," Mrs. Simpkins supplied.

"She... Aunt Gemma said..." interrupted Mary, whom Nora realized had still been struggling to recall more details, as asked. "She said the man had black hair and 'is face had scars on it."

"Do you remember if there was anything else?" Nora asked gently.

"I am not sure, miss. I think she also said 'e was tall. I tried to remember what she said. The woman trembled so, I dinna wish to press 'er. Even though we were inside the door, she kept looking over her shoulder."

"Thank you, Mary. That description should help immensely." Nora noticed that the maid had begun to fidget, perhaps also shaken by the occurrence.

"I will get Mr. Woods, ma'am," offered Mary. Without waiting for a reply, she shot up the stairs.

Nora saw a slow grin form on Mrs. Simpkins' face.

"Do you have something worth sharing?" she queried, half-smiling. "I would love some good news."

"No, Miss Mason. Well, maybe. I noticed them two being friendly to each other, 'tis all," she answered.

"Ah. Thank you for telling me. As long as their work does not suffer, I cannot see any reason to forbid a friendship," Nora answered, considering each word as she spoke and hoping she was not making a mistake. However, she saw naught wrong with couples in the same employment. Decisions seemed harder when more people's lives were involved.

Moments later, Nora heard footsteps approaching the parlor and stood up to see who it was, on the chance it could be two of the older children. Amos Woods opened the door and Mary followed him into the room. Nora bit her bottom lip at the look of adoration on Mary's face. A small pang of regret struck her at the realization she might never experience such a feeling toward a man.

"Miss Mason, Mary said you needed me, ma'am."

"Yes, Woods. I have just received some startling news. We have fourteen children here and they are all dear." Nora drew in a deep breath to calm her nerves. "One of those children, little Amy, may need to be watched closely. I have received a note which appears to threaten her position here. A man calling himself Mr. Sneed claims to be Amy's father. I do not know a delicate way to put this, except to say that Amy's mama could not say who the father was, and therefore, Mr. Sneed cannot know either. Her last wish was that Amy be given a chance at a better life, and we are charged to do that." She turned to Mary and Mrs. Simpkins. "If you see anyone strange loitering outside the house—even across the street, watching it, please make sure you bring the children inside, lock the doors and alert Mr. Woods and me. I will not have *my* children snatched to learn street trades in the East End," she finished, almost out of breath.

Nora had not realized how upset she had become over this note.

She cared for the little girl and would, somehow, see her with a better future. She needed to visit her grandmother. Grandmama would have ideas about how to deal with this additional problem. However, what Nora really needed was answers about the deed. "I shall return in a couple of hours. If you have need of me, a message will find me at Countess Whitton's townhouse," she added as she began to put on her pelisse and hat.

"Yes, ma'am," Woods responded. "I will take a look around the house now and make sure the windows are secure."

"That is a good idea. I had not even thought of that. Thank you."

The servants left the room and checking her hat and pelisse in the room's mirror, Nora picked up her reticule before walking to the front door. As she was about to open it, there was a knock. The pulse in her throat pounded as she peered through the small peephole. She was momentarily relieved it was a familiar face and opened the door. A completely different tension overtook her—one she was thoroughly unaccustomed to. With a start, she realized was attracted to this man. That only complicated her pique.

Lord Shefford removed his hat and gave an elegant bow. "I believe there may be a few details to discuss, Miss Mason. I apologize for arriving unannounced. You were just leaving." He said the last as he observed her apparel.

"Lord Shefford, good morning. I was leaving to visit my grandmother. To what do I owe the pleasure?" she said, smiling tightly and trying to regain the composure this last hour had taken from her.

"I think it is important that we talk now," he said coolly, arching a brow. "May I?" He pushed past her and nodded towards the parlor. Without waiting for a reply, he opened the door and walked into the room.

CHAPTER 9

*C*olin immediately noticed Miss Mason's crossness, but it did not signify. He had much more important matters on his mind. He sought to have this pact over with soon so his life would return to normal, and that meant *without a wife*. Bergen was right. Countess Whitton had bested him in the bargain. It would give him great pleasure when he could return to the calculating Countess and collect the debt her son owed him—unencumbered by a wife.

For now, he would do as she asked.

"May we talk?" Colin asked, ignoring the huff of impatience the woman expelled behind his back.

"As you seem to believe we are about to discuss something, I will attempt to give you my full measure of attention," she remarked in a severe tone.

He fought not to smile. It was too easy to rile Miss Mason. Sparring with her was enjoyable. Who knew? Perhaps there could be some redemption in this two-week interlude, he thought, catching himself gazing into very expressive, chocolate-brown eyes.

"I recognize the distraught manner of your appearance. May I be of assistance?"

"I appreciate your keenness. I will be well enough, sir. However, I wonder at the urgency you must feel, having rushed past me," she said acerbically.

He narrowed his eyes. "I see that I have not made a good impression on you. I would like the opportunity to correct that. Might we start again?"

"No, thank you," she snapped. "I expect ours to be a perfunctory connection, Lord Shefford, and therefore I feel no need to begin again, as you request. You arrived, unannounced, to tell me you had won my orphanage in a bet and all but made me feel I should immediately pack my bags and those of the children. Before I can even verify that to my satisfaction, here you are again." She narrowed her eyes and took a cleansing breath. "Pray, tell me at once your most urgent need to meet with me which keeps me from my business."

He deserved that, Colin admitted to himself. His civility with her had been the bare minimum to non-existent, recalling that he just barged past her—a poor display of behavior which had not been his intention. Still, she could be the most infuriating of women. How had winning one game drawn him into such a predicament? He reminded himself that he needed to rub along with her for two weeks. "While sparring with you gives me much amusement, Miss Mason, I would seek a better level of understanding. I have a proposal for you."

"A proposal?" she tittered. "What kind of proposal? I understood it was a foregone conclusion that the orphanage would be displaced because of my uncle's loose morals."

"That was my first thought, I will admit. However, I see that you are especially attached to this place." He looked around the room. "I have done some research, and it seems this was a very popular orphanage in years past. Many of the children that lived here have gone on to make sizeable contributions to society." He considered the meeting with the Countess as research, he reflected with some slight malice.

A smile formed on her face then, Colin noticed, despite her best efforts to suppress it. *I hope she does not call me on this.* He was on thin ice, unsure why he had fabricated such a tale, except that it seemed important to give her one rubber at least.

"What do you expect to achieve with this, Lord Shefford?" she questioned, remarkably with less hostility in her voice than before.

Good, I have her interest. "My proposal is that I come fairly regularly for a fortnight. I will be a willing participant in the day-to-day operations. My aim is that you prove to me that this orphanage has more chance of success in this building than the business I had in mind." He noted her face, particularly the irritation flickering in her brown eyes. The hostility had returned.

"*Lord Shefford.*" She emphasized his surname with a hint of distaste. "That is a preposterous proposal—and it is a colossal waste of my time, for I am doomed before I begin. You do not have a reputation for charity, and I cannot imagine you deciding anything in my favor. You and your friends seemed both surprised and disgusted to find this building occupied when you arrived the other day." She drew a slow breath. "Before I decide, I would invite you to meet some children the move would displace."

"Certainly. To show you my sincerity, I would be happy to meet a few of your charges."

"There are fourteen," she challenged.

"Fourteen," he concurred. "Where are they?"

"You shall meet one or two of them any moment now, unless I miss my guess." At her words, Alice and Amy scurried into the room, accompanied by Mary.

"Miss Mason, Alice has something important to tell you," Mary blurted out as she came in, giving a quick curtsey. Alice stood very still, squeezing a cloth in one hand and holding tight to Amy's little hand with the other. She had a thumb in her mouth.

"What do you have to say, Alice?"

"I was looking out o' the window and there were a tall man out on the street. A scary-looking man," the child said, her voice wavering from fright. "I seen him before. He was near me old house."

"Alice…" Nora pulled the child closer against her skirt. "I promise to do everything in my power to keep that man away from you—all of you."

69

"Mary told us you would keep us safe," she said, sniffling from tears.

"Who is this man?" Colin asked from behind, pushing down annoyance at having to reassert his presence.

With an exaggerated sigh, Nora turned to him. "I will have to tell you in a few minutes."

Something in her eyes told him she could not speak of it in front of the children.

"Who are these pretty little girls," he persisted, crouching down to their level.

Miss Mason gave him that questioning and exasperated look she seemed to have perfected. Admittedly, she challenged him more than any other female had ever done before, and found it amusing. He also found her intelligence stimulating, and imagined loosening the tight chignon that bound her blonde mane.

"Lord Shefford, these curly-headed beauties are part of our family. This is Alice," she said, nodding to the taller one, "and this is Amy." The smaller child turned and hid her face inside the folds of Miss Mason's skirt.

Still crouching, he leaned over and held his hand out to Amy. "My name is Lord Shefford, but you have leave to address me as Uncle Colin," he said, thus reminding himself he was not on a first name basis with Miss Mason. "It is nice to meet you, Amy, and you, Alice." He observed that Alice was scrutinizing him closely.

"You don't look nasty like that other man," she offered as she took his hand.

"Miss Mason..." He looked up at her. "I feel the need to learn more about this man. He has upset the children greatly and that will not do at all." He turned to Alice. "Where did you say you saw him?" He really wanted to know. He would not have a criminal sort watching these children. There could be a need for more security.

"I will show you, my lord," Miss Mason interrupted brusquely. "First, let me help Mary get these two sweetings off to bed. 'Tis been a while since they ate. They need a wee nap."

He watched Miss Mason pick up Amy and hold her close, cooing to her as she walked the girls away. Alice held her free hand. Suddenly, he realized he had been there almost an hour and still had not struck the bargain that the Countess had asked of him. Annoyed with himself, he determined to do so when Miss Mason returned.

A few minutes later, she walked back into the room.

"Your day has varying levels of unpredictability to it," he offered in solicitous tones, "and yet you do not believe my sincerity."

She stared at him. "You are quite right. I wonder at your surprise, sir. After the way we met, and the proposal you have, with such *grace and consideration,* just proffered, I cannot believe you to care. Nevertheless, I appreciate your kindness to the children."

"Did you think I was just being kind for show?" His chest lifted with indignation. Catching himself before he uttered an unforgivable retort, he swiftly composed his features. "I beg your pardon. I truly wish to help. What can you tell me about the man?" Colin realized he was sincere. He was genuinely concerned for this woman and her children.

"Very well, if you insist," she sighed. "I received a note earlier from a friend of Amy's mother. When Amy's mother died, leaving the child alone, this woman brought her to us. Amy knows her as Aunt Gemma." She fished in her reticule and withdrew a note, passing it to him. "This note says a man is trying to claim Amy. However, Gemma is certain he is not the child's father. *I believe her*. Hearing Alice say she has seen him, confirms it for me."

"In the eyes of the law, fathers have rights," he said calmly. "I would like to have this man investigated. If he means Amy, Alice or any of the other children harm, I will ensure we keep him away from the premises."

"How can *you* stop him?" she asked. "If Gemma and Alice are right, this is a man who could not care a straw for the law. And he has already located Amy. He aims to take her away from me, I know it." Her voice rose to a high pitch.

"Your grandmother is a countess and a powerful figure in Society. How can you ask me that?" He could not prevent the jeering tone. "You may recall, I am an earl."

"I do not rely on my grandmother, and since I have little or no involvement with the *ton*, I am not familiar with the power of an earl," she responded tartly.

"Does all this mean you need my help?" He found himself becoming irritated with the minx, *again*! "What is it about my proposal that you find so offensive? Is there any likelihood of our coming to a mutual agreement?"

"In a word, sir—*no*. That is not to say I do not welcome your help. However, as far as the proposition goes, I fear that would not be possible, sir. We both know the orphanage is merely your momentary charity. Something new will claim your attention and you will be away!" She waved her hands in a sign of irritated display. "To you, this... *my orphanage*... is only a building, a trophy for your winnings." She actually glared at him. "Now, if you will forgive me, I must be on my way. Is there anything else?" She retrieved her hat, which had *somehow* found its way to the hall tree, placed it on her head without recourse to a mirror and picked up her reticule.

"That is palpably untrue. I came here in the spirit of friendship in the hope we could work together, for a short period, in order that I might learn more," he argued.

"Not that it is any of your business," she said scathingly, pulling on her gloves, "I am off to visit my grandmother—if you will but allow me to leave."

This woman was dismissing him! Up until now, Colin had been doing his utmost to control his temper, but suddenly he had had enough. He had never met a woman so infuriating.

Without thinking, he snapped, *"If I asked you to marry me, would you take that seriously?"* Colin stiffened as the words left his lips, his mind absorbing what he had just done.

The room became quiet; starkly quiet. For a long moment she eyed him curiously. Putting down her reticule, she spoke in a composed voice.

"I accept."

CHAPTER 10

I *have just accepted a proposal of marriage.* The impulsive side
of her had responded when she heard the words, his offer
something she had never thought to hear from anyone. She was
certain he had asked her, although she could not imagine *why. Is it*
real?

A curious reaction bubbled up inside her. She wanted to laugh and
cry at the same time. It would not be a love match, as she had always
wanted. The gentleman was very handsome, she admitted, especially
when he became flustered. If she was being honest with herself, she
felt energized in his presence and enjoyed the interchanges, terse as
they were. There was a level of excitement she could not deny—
abruptly astonished to realize she had become focused on his lips.

Nora started to speak, to say she had made a mistake—anything to
unbind her from this man—yet she did not. As she thought about it, it
was the perfect solution. Marriage to Lord Shefford could be the
complete answer. She would have the protection of his name—whatever that meant—and perhaps she would have the financial wherewithal to save these children, if he agreed. She might also be able to
create an opportunity for a stream of revenue, through charitable
contributions, to support a place for single women to live, as long as

they held a paid position. *It could work.* Still, marriage was a leap in the dark. Nora realized her imagination was doing leaps and bounds of the same magnitude. Nonetheless, she could not deny herself. Marriage, children of her own, a home and a loving husband were all things she had imagined having… just not with a member of the *ton*.

What would Mama and Father have to say about it? I suspect Grand-mama will be over the moon.

"Did you say, *you accept*?" Lord Shefford had paled to the color of whey and looked so dumbfounded Nora was hard put not to laugh.

"I did indeed. It seemed the most reasonable proposition you have put forth this day," she acknowledged, pleasantly. "I will admit to being surprised by your offer."

"You are not alone," he muttered, his voice almost too low for her to hear.

Nora was obliged to bite her tongue to hold her humor at bay.

"I beg your pardon? I did not quite catch what you said," she commented in the sweetest of voices as she once more removed her gloves and hat. She could not forsake her betrothed at this most romantic of moments, she thought cynically.

"I said, I meant it," he replied.

His mouth spoke the words; however, his eyes registered what Nora could only determine as shock.

"Are you quite certain, my lord?" As she offered him a chance to back out, it occurred to her that maybe she was rather giving herself a chance to renege.

"Quite certain, my dear." He cleared his throat. "I do not suppose you would stay and discuss one or two matters with me before you leave for your grandmother's house, would you?"

He almost sounded as though he were pleading. "I will be happy to, my lord," she returned. "I am not the girl to accept an offer of marriage and then leave the gentleman in the lurch." Nora's brain screamed at her to stop talking. She had locked herself into this betrothal. She glanced at Lord Shefford and noticed he was staring at her with a curious look on her face.

"Since we are now betrothed, I should dearly like to know what you are thinking…" he started.

"Indeed? I fear my thoughts are quite jumbled. I have no notion why you asked me to marry you. We barely know each other; in addition, our exchanges have been less than amiable."

"We can change that," he mumbled, moving closer.

She savored the fresh essence of bergamot that his nearness brought, yet was a little shocked by the curious reaction it caused. Perhaps it was the excitement of this day so far, she mused. Suddenly nervous of what it all meant, she fought against an impulse to swoon and instead, gazed into his face, finding herself transfixed by the movement of his lips.

"I can admit to my astonishment at having," he said lazily, "proposed… so quickly. However, I cannot regret it." He tilted her chin up with his finger.

Her heart began to pound as strangely familiar pulses of pleasure shot down her neck and across her shoulders the second he touched her face.

"As we have just become betrothed, I am inclined to seal the proposal with a kiss." Without waiting for her agreement, he slanted his head and captured her lips with his.

At first, Nora was speechless. Yet his lips felt so soft and wonderful. He pulled her closer and a strange headiness took over her senses. *This kiss!* Nora had known nothing like it in her life. She craved more. A sense of need thrilled and overwhelmed her. She relaxed and circled her arms about his shoulders, fingering the dark brown curls at the base of his neck. Nothing she had known had prepared her for this. He nipped gently at her closed lips and she opened them to admit his tongue, which swirled around her own and touched the sides of her mouth seemingly to gain her participation. Nora could not resist the temptation he offered and met his tongue with her own, dipping and swirling together as if in a dance. Their breaths mingled with a ferocity she had never imagined. Everywhere his hands touched, even merely sliding down her arms, sent incredible bolts of sensation to her core. She savored the stir her body was experiencing and wanted to stay in this moment forever, but propriety dictated…she stop.

Half-heartedly, she pulled back. They both stood there, panting.

"I apologize…" he said before breaking off.

"No, please… There is no need to apologize. I… have never been kissed before… of course… and… I-I would not wish such… such a first kiss not to have been meant," she whispered, obviously shaken.

"I was not apologizing for kissing you," he said. "I was merely about to express my regrets for not having kissed you sooner."

Her heart gave a little flip.

They stared at each other, neither speaking for some moments.

"I plan to spend time here and see how an orphanage—this orphanage—operates. I wish to understand more," he finally said. "Will you allow it?"

"Did… did you mean what you said, then? Your proposal—the one you presented before you made your declaration of marriage?" she asked. Her voice was barely audible. She could tell, before he said a word, that he *had* meant it.

He nodded.

Regret stirred throughout her body. She had barely listened to him and had snubbed him whenever he had tried to speak. Yet, his tone had remained that of a gentleman. *Have I misjudged him?*

"I-I rather liked it," she admitted with a little more voice, feeling heat rise in her cheeks.

"You have me at a disadvantage. *What* did you like?" he asked.

"Your kiss," she murmured. The heat scorched her face at her brazen words. She lifted her chin and met his gaze, refusing to be missish. "If truth be known, sir, I enjoyed your kiss very much." *What was it about this man? It was as if her mouth said things without her brain's permission.* She craved his closeness. Why was one taste not enough? She had worked herself into a lather over his winning the building, and because of that, had tried her best not to pay him any heed. To make matters worse, she had felt forced into an impossible position because of the man who threatened Amy. Having a gentleman to take care of her made sense, and while she was not in disagreement with her decision, it went against all she had *thought* she desired.

"Perhaps we should talk," he prompted.

"I presume you mean about our engagement?" Her brazenness stunned her — yet, there were questions that needed answers. What kind of marriage would theirs be? She wanted to know what he expected but was unsure how to broach the subject.

"Yes, although there is more we should discuss than just that. Would you consent to accompany me on a drive in the Park tomorrow? I could take you up at ten of the clock."

A lump had formed in her throat and her voice rasped when she spoke. "Very well," she answered simply.

He inclined his dark head and a smile creased his face. "It is arranged. Now, tell me everything you know about this Mr. Sneed. We need to look into this matter. And I would very much like to meet the other twelve children."

She studied his face and was sure a look of incredulity must have stolen across her own.

"You are sincere! You would help me, even after I ignored everything you said earlier?"

He chuckled. "You *did* do that," he said, a meaningful look in his eyes. "However, I never offer anything which I do not wish to give." He edged nearer.

She sensed he was as surprised by his offer as she had been. *I never offer anything which I do not wish to give.* His words played over in her head and gave rise to that peculiar burst of excitement fluttering deep within her stomach. Nora looked up and saw only his lips as they unexpectedly claimed her own.

This time, their kiss was softer. As he pulled her close, she relaxed into it immediately. A tingling sensation shot across her arms and down her neck to her toes.

His hands encircled her waist and drew her even nearer, as his tongue gently swirled about the warm caverns of her mouth. Entranced, she fingered the waves of his hair. His caresses stirred feelings she had never known. *Was this desire?*

"You smell delicious. Is that honeysuckle?" he murmured, capturing her earlobe with his teeth. Then, nuzzling her neck, he dusted kisses along her collarbone.

Nora started to speak but was immediately lost in the sensations aroused by his kisses along the neck of her gown. Time stood still, until rapid steps in the hall awoke her senses, reminding her where she was.

"*Yes... oh good heavens!*" Nora drew a quick breath. "I confess, I find myself muddled by your nearness, sir. My good sense seems to have left me," she said. Her hands slipped from his shoulders and she stepped away.

The door opened, and Mrs. Simpkins hesitantly stepped inside. "Miss Mason, we have a situation."

"*A situation?* Whatever has happened?" Her face crinkled in concern, she briefly regarded Lord Shefford.

Mrs. Simpkins wrung her hands. "Miss Mason, I apologize for the interruption. That man is back."

"He is here, *now?*" Lord Shefford demanded as his eyebrows shot up.

"Aye," she said in a tremulous voice.

"Can you point him out to me?" he persisted.

"I saw him, m'own self, m'lord, staring at me from outside the kitchen window. His face were pressed to the glass. Right fierce it were." Mrs. Simpkins waved her hands and then nervously wiped them on her skirt and anxiously led them towards the dimly lit kitchen. "I was about to start the ovens for supper. Something made me look up... and there he were. A big, ugly fellow he was, sir." She pointed with a shaking hand towards the offending window. "It near frightened me to death. Soon as he saw I'd seen him, the ugly rascal ran towards the woodshed, over there by the big elm tree. I dropped me soup pot and all me beans went everywhere," she lamented.

Lord Shefford glanced at Nora, before walking to the back door and opening it. "I do not see him. Where did you say he was standing?"

Mrs. Simpkins hesitantly stepped towards the window and peered outside. "He was right there... I don't see him now, my lord," she whispered. "He was so close he could see me own icy breath in this room, and I could see his." She leaned down and unsteadily picked up her soup pot and placed it in the sink.

"Could you more fully describe him to me, Mrs. Simpkins?" Lord Shefford asked, his voice soothing.

"M'lord, he was tall and looked cruel. His hair was dark, and I think his eyes are black. Big black eyes they looked." She puffed out a tremulous breath before continuing, "His face has pimply scars and a black mustache."

Lord Shefford stepped back inside the room, looking around. "I believe you, Mrs. Simpkins. Where is Woods?"

"I expect he has gone back upstairs to work on the classrooms." Nora spoke up.

"I came straight away to find you, Miss Mason," the housekeeper added.

"Thank you, Mrs. Simpkins. I will see what can be done. Please fetch Woods and ask him to look around the premises. Do as Miss Mason suggests and keep the children within sight." He turned to Nora. "Unless I am wrong, this man has determined that the orphanage offers more than one opportunity. I know the fear you feel is for little Amy. However, I would suggest you treat all the children as if they are in danger. I think you are safe for now."

Luckily, the younger children were taking a nap and the older ones were practicing their letters, so she did not have to worry about their whereabouts. Saying nary a word, Nora listened cautiously. Lord Shefford had become protective. *He cares.* There was still so much that she needed to ask him, but the orphanage and the children were vastly more important to her. She bit her lip and inclined her head, refusing to allow her own nerves to show.

"There are things I can do to help. Nevertheless, there is only so much I can do while here. Although I need to leave, I will return. Might I have a few moments of your time before I go, Miss Mason?"

She turned to Mrs. Simpkins. "Please make sure the latches on the doors and windows in the kitchen are fastened securely. Keep the light down. I will come down shortly, to assist you."

"Yes, Miss Mason."

Nora did not miss the small iron frying pan the cook held within her skirts. Barely holding in an inopportune giggle, she remarked:

"I can see you are well-armed."

"Yes, ma'am. The man looked like the Devil himself, with eyes black as coal. I don't intend to let him near our little Amy."

"I am certain you will acquit yourself well with the frying pan, should the challenge present itself," Nora responded, her voice as solemn as she could muster. "I will accompany Lord Shefford to the door."

She and Lord Shefford walked in silence to the front entrance.

"I plan to return later with more men, Miss Mason." His eyes glimmered, challenging and teasing her. "And I would like to meet the other children."

She nodded, unable to speak and suddenly unsure of what to say.

"I would ask that you call me Colin, as we are now betrothed," he added, leaning closer.

Nora worried her bottom lip. The man's nearness excited and flustered her. Shyness gripped her throat as she struggled to speak.

"You may call me Nora... Colin," she said, looking into his eyes. Would he kiss her? *She hoped so.*

He leaned forward, but just as quickly, pulled back again. An easy smile spread across his handsome features.

"I am sincere about my offer. May we speak of it tomorrow?"

"I would like that." She reached into her pocket and withdrew the note she had placed there in what now, seemed an eon ago. "Here. Take this with you. It is the note we received this morning, about Mr. Sneed. You may need it." *I trust him.* She could not have imagined such a thing only a day ago—or even this morning. Truthfully, *no one* could have imagined any of this. "Thank you."

He placed the note in his pocket and tugged her closer. "This is a different side to you," he observed. "I enjoyed the fiery side, but this new side is nice. I find I want to know you better." His eyes blazed down at her. "I would like to kiss you once more."

She could not resist and softly lifted onto her toes, moving her arms about his neck as his mouth covered hers. A now familiar flutter shot down her spine to her center, eliciting a small shiver.

"Are you cold?" he murmured, his lips hovering above hers.

She gave a slight shake of her head, her eyes fixed on his. "This is the warmest I have ever felt in my life," she whispered.

CHAPTER 11

$\mathcal{C}$olin took the steps to his front door two at a time. Franklin opened the door for him to pass through and accepted his gloves, hat, and cape as he entered.

"My lord, Lord Bergen awaits you in your study. He has just arrived," the retainer said.

"Thank you, Franklin." Colin turned. "Please send a footman to my study. Send Davis. I have a task which needs to be done quickly. Wait," he interrupted himself. "Send Davis and two more footmen."

"Yes, my lord." The retainer bowed. "At once."

His mother's laughter tinkled from upstairs and Colin shook his head as he hurried to his study. He would never tire of the sound of her laugh. It warmed him. Mother would dearly love the tangle he had just created for himself, he knew, yet he had no plans to tell her. Wisdom dictated he first accepts it himself. Try as he might, he could not regret it. Swiftly walking into the room, he moved behind his desk and picking up the decanter of brandy from the library table, poured himself a healthy measure. He swallowed it when he heard Bergen's voice behind him.

"What has given you such a thirst?" he asked with dry humor.

He turned slowly, a smile stretched across his face. *I walked right past him. How did I miss him?* Franklin had mentioned Bergen was here, yet with his own preoccupation, Colin had forgotten—in the space of a few strides!

"I came to see how you were progressing. I was on my way to the club and waited for you," his friend said, his voice full of mirth. "You look as if your attention is elsewhere."

"*Damnation!* I cannot go with you. This day has not gone as I would ever have imagined." He picked up a second glass from the silver tray and poured a generous amount for his friend, passing it to him as he refilled his own. "Congratulate me, Bergen. I should get this over with."

"Congratulate you?" Bergen raised an eyebrow in amusement. "You had my full attention at *damnation*. I am listening." His eyes glittered with enjoyment as he raised his glass and took a small sip.

"I should start from the beginning. However, I do not have time; and I need your help," Colin responded. "I am engaged. I also need to hire a good Bow Street Runner."

Bergen spat out a small amount of the brandy as he struggled to sit up straight. "Wait! Who? What? Can we go back to the beginning?"

"Miss Mason..." Colin started before breaking off, certain of the ridicule he would suffer.

"How did that happen?" Bergen sniggered.

"Hush! Mother is upstairs. I have no wish to have her join this discussion." Colin felt heat rise past his ears.

"*Hear what*, my son?" A swish of silks and taffeta accompanied her query as his mother glided in and took the chair in front of his desk. "Thomas, I was unaware you were here. It's always good to see, you, my dear. Did I hear you say Miss Mason's name?"

He was well and truly caught, mired in mud up to his waist with nowhere to go.

"Mother. To what do I have the pleasure?" he asked politely.

"Whisht! Do not distract me. I wish to hear more about Miss Mason." She waved at him. "Tell us at once."

He turned away, unwilling to watch their faces. This was not like him. Hell! This day had been like no other he could recall. To top it off, he felt a burning need to return to the orphanage. "I asked Miss Mason to marry me," he said in a low voice, turning slowly. Two shocked faces stared back, both gaping rudely. The silence was deafening.

"You appear displeased, Mother," he quipped. "I thought you, of all people, would be happy." His tone was sarcastic and at once was ashamed. Mother did not merit that.

She walked to him and hugged him, her arms about his neck. "I am thrilled. However, I am rather taken aback. When did this happen?"

"I apologize for my tone, Mother. There was no need for that." He kissed her on the cheek. "I am as eager to review the details as you are to hear them. Yet I beg you will allow me to do that later. My... b... betrothed..." He stumbled over the word before moving on. "...is in trouble and I need to assist her." Clearly, becoming accustomed to his new circumstance would take time.

"This was a 'gallant knight' type of engagement then, was it?" his mother said, her expression radiating pleasure. "I rather like it. There are so many possibilities."

Colin turned to Bergen, who still sat in stunned silence. "I can see I must say more." He sipped his brandy, hoping for fortification. "I was trying to carry out the Countess' wishes in order to gain my winnings. Miss Mason was not compliant. We argued, and the next thing I knew, I had proposed. She accepted before I even comprehended my words."

"Whew!" Bergen whistled. "I would never have guessed such a turn of events. You have won yourself a beautiful lady with a brain to boot. You shall never be bored." Now grinning widely, he returned his drink to the tray and stood up. "I offer my heartiest congratulations," he said, extending his hand. "Did she run?"

"Is that why you need the Bow Street Runners?" his mother enquired in a neutral tone.

"I suppose you both think yourselves very funny." His mother and Nora shared a quick humor. "You should enjoy Nora's wit. I find her verbal sparring very attractive." Colin realized his affliction today, for saying things unchecked by his brain, was continuing. But strangely, he realized he liked the sound of her name on his tongue and acknowledged a warm feeling he felt when he thought of her. "There is danger afoot, and I need to return to Nora and the children. A man is trying to claim one of the smallest children, whose mother passed away in a drugs den. The child is but a toddler. He is watching the orphanage. The household servants have reported seeing him twice. I want to protect them and find this villain."

"*Good God, man!* Trouble continually follows that bet with Whitton," Bergen exclaimed.

Thankfully, Bergen did not elaborate on the wound he had suffered. "It does," Colin agreed. "As you will realize, I am sure, I had had no intention of offering for her. Quite the opposite, in fact. It was quite extraordinary; it was as if I was witnessing the event from without my own body." He chuckled. "Yet, I cannot say I am sorry," he added hastily. "I find her passionate and engaging, and as I will eventually have to pick a wife, this lady will never bore me."

His words met with disapproval from his mother, who was glaring in his direction. Father and Mother had been a love match.

"I apologize again for the unfeeling remark, Mother. I understand it will not be the marriage you have always envisioned for me." His mother had always wished the same for him and had never engaged in chicanery or other means in an attempt to leg-shackle him as he had seen happen with other *ton* friends.

"My son, ideas and circumstances change. I am happy to be of help," she answered, with a gleam in her eye.

"Good. The first thing I would ask is that you stay here so I will not worry about you. I have men searching for Whitton. The man is desperate, and I vow he will regret what he did to your house."

She bobbed her head in agreement. He paused, expecting her to leave the room, but to his surprise, she stayed where she was. Moments later, Davis entered with two other footmen.

"Perfect timing, Davis. I need you to find John Pelling of the Bow Street Runners. Check the office in Bow Street and his home. Tell him I wish to see him as soon as possible." Colin looked past Davis at the two footmen who had followed him into the room. "Both of you report to one Amos Woods at this address," he said, scribbling the address of the orphanage on a piece of paper. "You are to keep the location secure. Although two men work there currently, they need more help. A tall, dark-haired rogue is threatening the children. I believe he means to snatch them to work on the streets. We need to keep them safe." Behind Colin, his mother sucked in a deep breath at his remarks.

"Does the Countess know of this?" she inquired.

"Not as yet. Nora—Miss Mason—was on her way to speak with her grandmother when I arrived," he replied.

"I have many questions. However, I stand ready to assist in any way needed," Bergen declared.

The two men watched in amused astonishment as his mother walked to the brandy decanter and filled a glass before retaking the seat next to Bergen.

"I believe you may afford me a few minutes to tell me about my future daughter-in-law. I would like to be of help—to both of you" she said, sipping her drink. "What manner of celebration will you allow me to plan?"

"Believe it or not, we have not yet discussed it. The activities of the orphanage have occupied us somewhat, and we have not spoken about it beyond my offer and her acceptance. The truth is, I was hoping to learn more about her family from you," Colin responded. "I can say that the engagement was a surprise to us both. I offered in a fit of pique," he admitted, standing and walking to the fireplace. He tossed a crumpled-up wad of paper into the low flames and watched it ignite before regarding his friend and his mother. "However, I find I cannot regret it. She gave me an opportunity to withdraw, and yet, I could not. I find her fascinating," admitted. *Was he smitten? No. That takes time, does it not?* In truth, he had no idea. Colin had never felt this way about any woman. He glanced at his friend for succor, but the smirk on Bergen's face told him nothing was forthcoming.

His mother regarded him for a moment before breaking into a smile that seemed almost giddy and clapping her hands.

"Dearest, I cannot wait to meet her. If she is anything like her grandmother or her mother, she will be a delightful and spirited young lady. Her mother has maintained very little involvement with Society and therefore, I do not know her daughter."

"You lost your temper and offered for her?" Bergen choked out the words with a peal of laughter. "I beg your pardon. I wait with bated breath for the details. I have always known your temper to be your weakness. I never expected it to be your salvation!"

"I cannot explain my actions." Colin fell silent for a moment. "I ask you both to reserve judgment." He realized that his protective nature had become fully employed with the woman to whom he was now betrothed. Perhaps that explained the overwhelming need to return to her today. He had promised to make the orphanage more secure.

He gave his mother a quick kiss on the cheek and walked towards the door. "I shall return once I ensure Nora and her charges are safe. The footmen should be able to keep things in hand until I have a Runner in place."

"I understand, my son. I will send for my maid and clothing, and make myself comfortable," He could tell she wanted to say more but chose not to. Instead, she took another swallow of her brandy. "Be off with you. Attend to your betrothed," she urged.

"I will follow you out, Shefford," Bergen added, also giving Lady Shefford a quick buss on the cheek. "It was good to see you, my lady."

"Thomas, see that you give Elizabeth and the children my best. I have every intention of gathering us all together before you leave for the country," she chided softly. "You have always been like another son to me. I cannot wait to see your family again."

The two men walked quietly to the door and retrieved their coats, hats, and gloves.

"Franklin, will you send for the carriage?"

"It already awaits you, my lord. I expected you would need it."

Colin looked at his butler and dipped his head. "Thank you. You never cease to astound me." Turning to Bergen, he continued, "I know you have questions. I can set you down at your townhouse and we may talk for a few miles, if you care to tie your horse to the back of the carriage."

"I accept your proposal," his friend replied buoyantly. He signaled for the footman waiting with his horse to secure her to the back of Colin's carriage. "Merry will enjoy the respite." Bergen climbed into the carriage and took the seat opposite Colin.

As the carriage lurched forward, he leaned across. "I am more than ready to hear the rest of this story," he said with a big grin on his face.

Colin chuckled. His mother was right… Thomas Bergen was like another brother. He had been his best friend for as long as he could remember. Neither had kept a secret from the other in all those years.

"There is no possibility you will wait to hear this with Morray, is there?" he suggested weakly.

"Not a chance, my friend." Bergen's lips twitched. "I plan to savor every word which comes from the gentleman who swore he would never marry."

CHAPTER 12

A SMALL APARTMENT IN EAST END...

"What do you mean, *he overheard you speak,* woman? You have told a man—a man who deals in children like cattle—where to find my... mother's orphanage?" A thick vein pulsed in Lord Wilford Whitton's neck and his bulbous nose flattened in rage. "Tell me again how you spilled my business to a stranger, and how you know this man!"

"I should ask you the same," the woman muttered, her voice barely audible.

"What did you say?" he roared, propelling his flaccid body from the chair beside her bed.

She stepped out of his path and moved to the window overlooking the street and stared outside at nothing.

"I swear, Lord Whitton, I did not know the man was lurking in the shadows. I had to find a place for the child. He already has a cough... that cough that small children get what crawl in chimneys. He would not survive a life like that. I 'ad to do something." Tears streamed down her face as she turned to face him.

"You took a *child* from the chimneys and moved it to the orphanage? To my mother's orphanage? My niece lives there!" he bellowed. "If something happens, they will blame me. My mother will never forgive me—she is not one to cross." He paced the small room.

"I am sorry..." Jenny Maven let her voice trail off. She had grown tired of Whitton's huffy attitude, and after all she had done for him. *A lord, indeed!* she thought acidly. Instead of finding a protector, she had trapped herself with this odious excuse for a gentleman. He still had not told her *why* he was here, and she had stopped asking. It no longer mattered. She had hoped he felt something for her, yet now knew he cared only for his own hide. A sigh escaped her.

"Did you say something?" he thundered. "My niece has two women and about a dozen children living there, and you tell a blackguard who would do them all harm where to find them?" He held her gaze. "I cannot trust you with any information."

"Is that so, your lordship?" Furious and no longer afraid, she walked right up to him and pointed her finger close to his face. "Keep your voice down. I have some pride, and I do not need everyone to hear us. As far as your niece and the children are concerned, do not pretend to care about anyone but yourself. And I might suggest you stop shouting, considering you may want no one to know you are here." To her surprise, he stopped blustering and stared, boring into her with obsidian eyes. "Yes. I took Benjamin there. *What of it?*" She refused to cower to this man.

"You *know* his name? Is he your bastard?" He squinted, and his mouth pulled into a sneer as he taunted her.

"What business would it be of yours, if he was?" She hurled the quickest response she could think of in return. Were he standing closer, she might have slapped him. He had repulsed her. Lord Whitton was not a handsome man. He looked utterly revolting, like a squat, red-faced toad. How had her life become so desperate that she had committed any of her time to *him*? Jenny resolved, at that moment, that Whitton would know nothing further about her life. "I did not know he had followed me." Her voice sounded calmer and more measured than she felt. She had not even considered the possibility. Realization of her carelessness sent shivers of fear quaking through her. It was likely the child she had tried to save was in danger, thanks to her stupidity. *If Sneed sees him, he will take him.* She had been nothing but stupid lately, starting with allowing this short wad of a man into her apartment.

"What business is it of mine?" he mocked. "The man is a murderer!" Whitton continued his rant as he paced the room. "He has no conscience. The children play only a small part in his evil deeds."

It was clear Whitton feared his mother's wrath. Guilt over her sharp criticism of him—even though it be to herself—made her consider the possibility that he cared for at least, *some* of his family. He blustered enough about each of them. She surely knew every member by now—at least, everything he felt was wrong about them. His niece was a spinster, and according to her uncle, it was because she shunned the *ton* and all it afforded her. Jenny could not imagine spurning such a glamorous existence.

His niece's father was a stupid man, according to Whitton. He could have appealed to his mother for funds to care for his family when the family business fell on hard times, yet pride had kept him from asking. And Jenny could not even start on the confused web of insults and attributes he directed at his sister, although it seemed he cared for her.

"You have placed me in a difficult position," he finally said. His voice sounded calmer.

"I have apologized. Do you not think I feel bad enough about it? I could have kept my suspicion my own secret and not shared it with you."

"There has been nothing else you should tell me about, has there?" he taunted again.

"Fret you not, my lord," she said with a firm note of sarcasm, adding untruthfully, "I have said nothing to anyone about you being here. I merely feel sorry about the boy—Benjamin. However, your being in this difficult position is of your own doing," Jenny derided, holding her hands on her hips. "Do not forget that. You stabbed a peer."

He started at her words, causing her to back away a step.

Pretending more courage than she felt, she caught his gaze. "Yes, I know what you did. You refused to tell me, and I stopped asking, but people talk hereabouts."

"What do you want with me, woman?" An edge had returned to his tone.

"Nothing," she heard herself say. "You could at least be agreeable. Other gentlemen treat their mistresses with…"

He cut her off. "*Mistress?* You think you are my mistress?" His entire body recoiled from her. "You are naught but a bit of muslin."

The cruelty of his words rendered her speechless. He had not called her his whore, *exactly*, but he might as well have done.

Before she died, her mother had made Jenny agree to better herself. "Jenny" she had said, "promise me that ye will do yer best t' find a life that ye can be proud of. M' own life has me dying of the pox. I'll ne'er see ye grown. Oi want more fer ye, child." Jane Maven died later that very night.

Jenny had promised her mother to do better, but the gambling hell and its vices had been too tempting for a young girl, already hungry and penniless. She drew herself up. Quaking at her knees, she knew she had to change her path, *now*.

"Perhaps you should leave. I have no standing with you, and I am not sure why I ever cared. You are a horrid man. *Leave now!* Go home to your wife."

"Stop talking, Jenny. I need to think."

His reversal in attitude made her head spin. "Did you hear me, Lord Whitton?" She fairly screamed his name. "I said, 'Go home!'"

"Perhaps there is still some advantage to be made with my mother." He spoke aloud, almost to himself, while pacing up and down again.

He had ignored her.

Benjamin had wormed his way into her heart. She desperately

needed to help him—*somehow*. Except, first, she needed to free herself of this man.

"I am an earl. I have a great deal of influence." She heard him say.

He was not listening to her at all. What mischief was Whitton planning now?

CHAPTER 13

"Miss Nora, here's ye chocolate and a couple o' pieces of toast, and a wee biscuit from the batch I jus' pulled from the oven. I thought ye could use the indulgence this morning after the night ye had," Mrs. Simpkins said, placing a tray down on the small table next to Nora's bed. "I thought as how, with the extra men about, ye would sleep better."

Nora had been lying there, awake, and when Mrs. Simpkins knocked, she sat up and stretched, holding back a yawn. She needed a stout dish of tea.

"I could smell your heavenly biscuits all the way up here," she said with a giggle. "Did I wake you last night?"

"Ye did, miss. I came in and ye were screaming. It sounded like ye were praying. I sat next to ye and smoothed yer hair back from yer forehead until ye calmed and were resting again. Ye kept mumbling about little Amy but never opened yer eyes. She slept soundly all night. I looked in on her when I left yer room." The older woman scanned the bedchamber. "I confess, I worried about ye."

Nora recalled the dream. She had been running for her life, holding Amy close to her. Growing tired, she had stepped behind a building to catch her breath when powerful hands pulled her backward. It was a man, but she could not remember a thing beyond that. Perhaps Mrs. Simpkins' soothing manner had finally coaxed her from the dream. She wondered if it had been a vision, as a chill of fear seized her and shook her to the core. Nora had experienced visions in the past and had never deciphered their meaning until she witnessed the same incident happen in life. This dream frightened her still. It had to be the dastardly Sneed chasing her. Certainty eluded her— maybe because the dream had ended too soon. She could recall nothing about the man who caught her and fought to quell her growing panic. Had it been Sneed?

Nora had expected to sleep better, knowing that the perimeter of the school was being watched by Lord Shefford's footmen and was secure. Her mother had always said that visions did not happen until the body and the mind were relaxed. A shiver ran from her spine to her toes. She would let no one take Amy—or any child. Yesterday's visit to her grandmother had been delayed. Today, she hoped, nothing would prevent her from seeing Grandmama to discuss the deed and other things which had transpired, still needing to tell her about her betrothal.

As she sat on her bed, reflecting on her dream and nibbling her toast, Uncle Wilford's face flashed across her mind. Gosh! It had been a long time since she had had a foretelling. Could this be a second one? Could he be in danger or was he stirring more trouble? She knew naught of what it might mean and shook her head to clear it. The sun had already been up an hour, and she was eager to see Amy and Alice.

She stepped to her wardrobe and withdrew her golden muslin. Pleased with her dress selection, Nora secured the hooks and buttons on the front before leaning down and pulling on her half-boots. Having finished dressing, Nora gulped down the last of her chocolate, gathered together the dishes and hurried with them down to the kitchen.

"'Tis good to spy ye up and about Miss Nora! The children have just settled down to breakfast," the cook said, peering over her shoulder from the sink. "Spending time with ye before they begin their lessons will put a smile on a few faces," she added with a wink.

"I fear I slept a little longer than I usually do, and I do not want to miss this time with them," she said as she set down the tray and hurried back towards the schoolroom.

As she headed up the stairs, male voices in the entry startled her. One she recognized as Amos Woods. She must remember to thank Grandmama for adding the handyman to the household. Having him watch the front door was helpful. Another male voice spoke then, and his husky tone relaxed her immediately. Colin had arrived! No gentleman had ever stirred as many feelings within her as this one. *Curious. Why is he here so soon?* Had she forgotten something? Their carriage ride was not until ten.

The previous evening, he had arrived in time to oversee the additional guards he had arranged. It was thoughtful of him to lend her the footmen. Four men and three women now made up the employees at the school. The topsy-turvy nature of the household struck her as funny, causing her thoughts to turn fanciful. It was quite obvious that Mary had set her cap at Amos Woods, who clearly returned the attraction, and their burgeoning friendship was exciting her own sense of longing for a close relationship. Of course, Nora had not shared that she and the handsome Lord Shefford were betrothed. Still, theirs was a convenient arrangement—not the connection her heart desired. If she were honest, her heart desired him for reasons she failed to comprehend.

That only left Mrs. Simpkins spouseless. She snorted. *Just supposing...? No, that is just nonsense.* Still, she could not deny the amusement. The matchmaking mamas of the *haute ton* would marvel at the success found under one inauspicious roof in less than one week's time.

Nora avoided going downstairs to meet the company, reluctant to squander her time, and certain Woods could handle whatever presented itself. Instead, she visited the children to see how they did. They had finished their early meal and according to the schedule; it was time for watercolor painting. Easels and stools were being placed about the room by the children. Mary had already mixed the paints and set out the brushes. Paper and a pile of smocks were on a table by the door, for the girls to pull over their dresses. The boys had aprons that her grandmother had thoughtfully supplied. The Dowager Countess was an avid supporter of the arts and made sure supplies were plentiful, even encouraging all the children to take part.

Nora had her own supplies at the ready and positioned her chair across from her easel, choosing the space in front of one of the tall windows which lined the outer wall. She moved the curtains out of the way to allow for more light.

"There you are!" Colin sauntered in sporting an impudent grin and gave her a quick bow. "I am here to do your bidding, my lady."

Her bidding? She had looked forward to spending an hour or two with Amy and the other children. Frustration welled inside her and she felt confused *why*. This man was everything that most women would clamor to claim. He was a gentleman; he was handsome and according to gossip, he was rich. She looked up and his grey eyes found her own brown eyes. As he held her gaze, she realized that what she had called grey was actually a very pale blue with silver flecks. His eyes held her captive. *Damn it. She wanted him, too.* Once again, he was taking over her plans.

"I am quite sure I have professed no bidding," she snapped. *What was it about this man that could make her eager to see him and also wish him elsewhere?* He looked hurt. She immediately regretted her short-tempered response but did not apologize.

"I can be a quiet observer," he coaxed. "I thought it a good time to meet the other children—perhaps get to know them a little." He studied her face. "I can see you had not expected me, so please allow me to apologize for not speaking of my intention last evening. However, I am serious about our bargain and if I am to uphold my part of the bargain, I need to understand everything about the orphanage, and that includes the beneficiaries." He regarded the room about them. "You are setting up for a class." It was an observation.

The state of annoyance kept her more alert and distant. Yet, despite her wariness, his unabashed honesty negated her efforts.

"Yes, I plan to start with simple painting techniques to see who has a talent for the subject. As a society, we expect girls to love art and endeavor to gain a certain skill. My own observations do not support that contention. Famous painters are usually men. We intend to give all the children a good basic education in reading, writing, and arithmetic. In addition, I think some tuition in the arts, and perhaps music, would give them an advantage in the world. My mother always told me that art encourages the finer ability to discern and read your surroundings. I feel the skill would be helpful to the children."

"You are sure it is wise?" His voice drifted off towards the end of the question.

Nora started to snap a retort, but sensed his comment seemed a more discarded thought than a proper question. The Earl had busied himself perusing the supplies, picking up the aprons, the papers, and looking at the table easels.

"I am heartened by your effort." As he spoke, his eyes remained focused on the children's efforts. "All the same, I fear you will need more paint and brushes. I shall have them delivered—paper, too. As I think about it, your reasoning makes sense. Children need to be alert to their environment, perhaps these children more than most, and if painting can aid that, so be it. You mentioned music." He paused and turned his head. "Do you have an instructor for that?"

Nora opened her mouth to respond and closed it before finally answering, "Eventually, my lord, I might do some rudimentary teaching using an older pianoforte. T'would be nice to have one in the parlor for small recitals, that is an aspiration only. There is so much more we need. Painting is our first endeavor." She still had much on her mind. Perhaps his wish to observe would, after all, not be too obtrusive. While a physical attraction between them felt more and more obvious to her, their ability to become contentious still existed, and she had no wish to have an argument in front of the children.

"Is my uncle in trouble?" she blurted out. Drat. She had meant to ask that with more propriety.

"I beg your pardon?" Colin's face wore a sudden formidable look. "Has something happened? Has he been here?"

"Your questions... and that look," she said, her skin prickling with alarm. "I feel there is something I do not know, yet I should. What might that be?"

The mention of Uncle's name appeared to create some level of concern, because Colin paused for a long moment before answering.

"Your uncle tried to kill me after losing this property to me."

She gasped.

"My friends and I have an idea where he is staying."

"Does my grandmother know?"

"She does." His voice was emotionless.

"I saw him." She instantly regretted her words, fearing his reaction to her gift.

He raised a brow. Nora was not sure how much to reveal, not wanting to be ridiculed. She enjoyed laughter, but not at her expense.

"I am prone to forewarnings, and his face flashed across my mind at the strangest of times this morning. I make it a habit *not* to think about my uncle, so I found it most odd." *I trust him with my feelings.* She discerned in that instant that her heart had begun to rule her head.

Showing only surprise, he did not laugh.

"I am interested in what you saw," he said, his voice softening. "My own mother has spoken of such presentiments. She has sworn many times that the fairer sex oft possesses the ability, and it should never be taken lightly."

"It was nothing more than that. 'Tis wholly unusual for me to even think about him. He has never been pleasant to my family, especially to my mother, his own sister."

Colin casually pulled up a brush from its holder and fingered it while he studied her.

"Your uncle has a... female companion... who lives in the East End, and we think he is staying with her," Colin informed her.

"A *ladybird*? I cannot imagine why she would ally herself with him, beyond the lure of his money." She heard herself disclose. She immediately regarded him. Had she shocked him? His expression remained calm.

"Uncle has never been pleasant to my mother or me, and my grandmother does not mention him. In fact, he is tight-fisted," she added. *Really, I must learn to guard my tongue. Whatever possessed me to tell him that, and in front of the children, for heaven's sake? I should know by now to keep my family business to myself.*

"Her name is Jenny Maven, and she is employed by the gambling establishment on the hill." He seemed nonplussed by her disclosure. She was unsure how she felt about *that*.

"Do you refer to *Lattimore Hill?*" There was little doubt what Uncle had been doing there, yet Nora wondered about Colin's presence at such a place. She wanted to ask, but a lady was supposed to know nothing of such establishments. Good sense this time kept her tongue in check. It was one more reason that she detested the *ton*. They went to places like East End and Seven Dials to mix with low company and visit the gin shops. It was not enough that the social classes were so abruptly dissimilar. Although the upper classes were aware of the needs of the poor, most turned a blind eye, their only concerns being to satisfy their own needs, and their own vices. Was there another attraction for him in the East End beyond gambling? "Do you intend to have him arrested?" Would it be too harsh to hope the answer to this was *yes?*

"Indeed. That is my plan. Still, I am pursuing some additional information before having him arrested. He has already bribed an official, for his release on the night of the incident, and is not aware we know where he is. Attempting to kill a peer is a very serious offense." He looked at her, his gaze holding hers.

To her surprise, she felt both pity and relief. The prospect of Uncle getting his comeuppance should thrill her considering how disagreeable he has been.

"What would you have me do?" he asked in a solicitous tone.

A fissure of contentment shot through her. Colin cared about her opinion. "You are in earnest? I would like to see him punished just enough to allow him to feel how he has made others feel," she ventured finally. The clamor of feet and the sounds of giggles sounded from the stairs. "Perhaps we should continue this later this morning, when we are in the carriage. The children are... coming... and here they are," she said brightly as the smaller children rounded the door-case and began eyeing the assembled art supplies. Amy and Alice made straight for her. "Sweetings, you recall Uncle Colin, do you not?" She caught his expression of amusement from the corner of her eye. *The energy she felt when in his presence was addictive.*

"Good 'ay, Uncle Colin," Alice said. The little girl gripped Amy's hand in hers. "Amy says good 'ay, too."

He chuckled. "I understand that you children are all going to turn your hands to painting today. I would very much like to watch, if that would be acceptable to you."

Nora and Colin looked about the schoolroom at nodding faces. "Well, it seems the children have spoken," she said—and even she could hear the smile in her voice. "Children, before we start, please find an overall. The girls have the smocks and the boys wear the aprons. Here are some for you younger children." She held out a few that would fit the smaller girls. There were no grumbles—not that she had expected any. She was fairly certain this was the first time most of these children had even seen supplies such as these, much less use them. "Everyone listen carefully, and I will show you how to begin. I want you to draw something that you like—anything you like," she told them clearly. Repressing a smile at the open mouths before her, Nora looked about the room and noticed Colin squatting down, talking to Becca. The little girl appeared to be drawing during their exchange.

Nora opened her mouth to say something, but chose instead to instruct the rest of the children so they might start. When she finished, she noticed Colin was still watching Becca draw, with few words being spoken. Satisfied that everyone could put something on the paper, she put down her brush and wiped her hands on her apron. Carefully edging nearer, she could hear their conversation.

"Is that a picture of your last home?" Colin's voice was gentle but laced with concern.

"Yes," she mumbled. "I lived with my aunt when my momma left."

"Who is that with you in the drawing?" he asked.

"It's my aunt and her friend."

Nora had heard enough. Coupled with the recent conversation she had had with Alice, it overwhelmed her curiosity. She quietly moved behind Colin and peered at the drawing taking shape in front of her. The dark-haired little girl was no stranger to paper and charcoal. Even though they were primitive, the faces held more detail than one might have expected from a child of seven. Nora recalled that there had been very little information about Becca and wished to know more. She noticed the drawing of a man with black hair and a mustache. Curious, she had to ask.

"Becca, my child, who is the man?" Nora inquired gently.

"Aunt Sarah said he was a friend." *What a curious statement*, Nora thought.

Becca looked up, her little face grimacing with concentration. "He said he was Aunt Sarah's beau."

"Do you recall his name?" She could not help persisting. *Can he be the same man? Impossible! You are grasping at straws, Honoria Mason.*

"She called him Tom when he was nice to her. He was mostly mean and caused her to cry a lot. When he was horrid, she would tell me to hide and not make a sound unless she called me. I heard someone call him Mr. Sneed. I am not sure, though." She looked back at her work. She had drawn a room with the three people standing side by side. The child had drawn herself looking away from Mr. Sneed.

Nora smiled and nodded. "That is a very good drawing, Becca. You have so much detail. Have you drawn before?"

"A little," she said quietly.

"Did your mother or your aunt show you how?" She noticed that the expression on Mr. Sneed's face was one of anger. He stood on the other side of what must have been her aunt. It was hard to miss the dark smudge on her aunt's arm. *Is that supposed to be blood?* She itched to ask, nonetheless resisting the urge, deciding not to stir a potentially painful memory.

"Aunt Sarah drawed a lot, and I watched her. Sometimes she would give me a piece of paper and a block of charcoal to draw with," she responded casually. "I had to put it in the woodpile when I finished."

Colin stood up and gave Nora a quick glance before returning his attention to Becca's drawing.

"May I ask what happened to your Aunt Sarah?"

"She died. Somebody found her floating in the river and said I had to leave before Mr. Sneed came for me. That's when they brought me here."

Nora gulped. Afraid to ask anything more about the picture, she changed the subject. "'Tis a perfect first effort, Becca." She looked around the room at the rest of the children working at their easels, some with more success than others. This morning's exercise had certainly been enlightening. Giving a hurried nod towards the door, she said, "Perhaps such a big effort deserves a surprise." As if on cue, Mrs. Simpkins entered, carrying a tray of small sandwiches, biscuits, and a pitcher of milk.

CHAPTER 14

*C*olin found himself both amused and alarmed by the various things he learned during his time with the children. The process made him more beguiled with Nora. His head swirled with thoughts of both her and the children. The drawings had been informative, and it had been joyous to watch them. Becca's drawing had been thought-provoking and sad. It had gripped his heart. Now he was standing next to a small, thin, blond boy who was drawing what looked like a chimney. Curious, he bent slightly over him to take a closer look.

To his surprise, the young boy looked up at him and smiled. "Good 'ay, Uncle Colin," he said in acknowledgment. "I ain't never met a fancy gentleman afore. You are a lucky cove to have yer own home."

Colin's heart immediately engaged with the child. "What are you drawing with your charcoal stick?"

"Miss Nora said to draw what we know. 'Tis a chimbley," he said, smiling.

"What inspires you to draw it, if I might ask," Colin persisted.

"I think it's because I wanted to look at it from this angle.

"What do you mean, *this angle*?" The boy and his talent intrigued

Colin. The child possessed a vivacity about him that made one happy in his company.

"'Tis so much nicer than from inside." The child grinned.

While he understood the darker meaning of what Benjamin had said, Colin smiled in return. The child seemed not to let his past dampen his mood.

"I can understand that lad." The boy's drawing stirred his interest. "What is your name?" he asked.

"They call me Benjamin, sir."

"Ah. That explains your picture more." A sadness gripped Colin's heart.

"I cleaned chimbleys afore I found my way 'ere," the small boy explained. "A lady what paid me to clean 'er chimney, tol' me I reminded her of someone she once knew. She was a nice lady and said I should not clean chimbleys and brought me 'ere. I gave it a chance, like she asked. Truth is, chimbleys made me feel bad. I like Miss Nora." Benjamin coughed—a dry hacking sound—almost as if it punctuated his point.

"That cough sounds painful. How long have you had that young man?" Colin asked, concerned.

"It comes and goes. Reckon I've had it fer a while, now," he answered, coughing into his shoulder. "The lady what rescued me tried to take care of it, too."

"I will speak to Miss Nora about it," Colin said, more for himself than for the boy. He would ensure a doctor saw Benjamin. That was something he could help with—and he knew the perfect doctor for these children. He should speak with Nora about it first, aware that he wanted her approval.

Reaching into his pocket, he withdrew his watch. It was almost nine o'clock. Colin looked around and realized Nora had already left the room. He had become so absorbed by Benjamin that he had failed to notice that the children had cleaned the room and prepared for their next activity. The discipline the women had instilled in these children, in such a short time, astounded him. He needed to take care of something.

"Benjamin, I have enjoyed talking with you and I look forward to spending more time in your company on my next visit."

"Thank you, sir!" he said, leaning down to scoop up a brush he had dropped.

On his way out of the orphanage, Colin saw Amos Woods. "Would you inform Miss Mason I plan to be back in an hour? And could you see that Mrs. Simpkins gets this note?" He wanted the afternoon to be perfect and felt sure the woman would help him with a few items.

"Yes, my lord." He heard the door click shut behind him.

Colin strode towards the stables and met his carriage, clearly startling his coachman, who had not expected to take him anywhere until ten.

"I wish to make a quick trip," he explained to the man, who, with the groom, scrambled to the coach.

"Very good, my lord. Where will we be going?" the groom asked, opening the door for him.

"Do you know where I may buy flowers and some confectionery in a hurry?" Colin directed the question to both men before he stepped into the carriage.

"I know just the place, my lord. 'Tis but a step from here," Gerard, the driver, returned before climbing into his seat. The groom closed the door and climbed aboard. Colin closed his eyes and settled back against the black leather squabs. He hoped he had enough time.

The sleek black carriage maintained a slow, yet steady pace to allow the coachman to navigate the cobble-stoned streets safely. Colin noticed the flower carts before he saw the small confectionery just beyond them.

This spot is perfect! He raised his cane to tap on the roof, whereupon the carriage stopped.

"My lord, I think you will find what you need here," the coachman remarked with a grin. "'Tis my mother's pastry shop. She makes the best marzipan in London."

"Your mother? This establishment belongs to your family?"

"Yes, my lord," Gerard replied, tipping his hat.

"How marvelous that you have brought me here! I have not had sweets in an age. I shall keep this confectionery in mind for future events, Gerard!"

Fifteen minutes later Colin came out with several packages tucked under his arm and a bag. Using his free hand, he purchased a large posy of yellow roses from a sidewalk cart vendor. Colin felt pleased with his purchases and happy that he had managed them so quickly.

"Your mother also had biscuits covered with nonpareils and taffy! I think I may have bought her entire stock. The children will be besotted with it!" He handed the flowers to his groom and arranged the packages, before reaching for the flowers.

"Yes, my lord. It is a certainty," his cheerful driver replied.

It seemed the carriage had barely started again before they were back in front of the orphanage. Colin shook himself from his bemusement. Still not able to fathom the workings of Miss Mason's mind, he hoped the flowers and confections pleased her. He wondered if any of the children had ever tasted candies or pastries. That thought weighed on him as he thought again of both Becca's and Benjamin's artistic efforts. That had been an easier goal before meeting some of these children. Their brief lives had been like nothing he could even imagine. Part of him was ashamed, realizing that such brief excursions into the East End as made by wealthy rakehell blades often left by-blows behind. It had been his plan to make this school into a fencing club. Sorrowfully, he wondered how many of these children had had such a beginning, considering it for the first time from a fresh perspective.

As he approached the steps of the house with packages in his arms, the door opened, and Nora came out onto the flags beneath the portico.

"I wondered where you had gone. Woods assured me you would return," she said with a nervous laugh.

"I hope you do not mind. A drive about Town could prove relaxing and would give us time to talk uninterrupted," Colin offered.

Her eyes opened wide in surprise. "What a wonderful idea."

The sound of hurried footsteps announced another's approach from behind her, and Nora stepped aside just as Mrs. Simpkins appeared, holding a small basket.

"My lord, here are the items you requested on your missive." Sporting a giant smile, the housekeeper pushed the covered basket into his hands.

"Thank you, Mrs. Simpkins. I appreciate this. I left too early this morning to have all of my thoughts properly collected, I fear." He chuckled. "These are for you." He pushed a small, wrapped package into her hands and closed her fingers about it.

The older woman swiped at her eyes. "That is so thoughtful, my lord," she enthused, fondling the small package. "'Tis a long time since a man gave me a gift!" She giggled.

"I cannot imagine you being overlooked," he said, beaming. "I hope you enjoy the gift. There should be enough sweets and marzipan in this larger package for everyone, especially the children." He passed a second parcel to her.

"Oh, the children will love this!" Mrs. Simpkins' excited tone brought a smile to Nora's face.

"Capital!" Colin had held back a small package, containing marzipan and the nonpareils, for their drive. "That is what I had hoped." He tipped his head and held out his arm. Nora placed her hand lightly on his arm, and he guided her to the carriage, helping her inside. After securing the basket underneath the seat, he sat down next to Nora. They were engaged, after all. It was their pending marriage that they needed to discuss, and he wanted as much as possible for the discussion to be in his favor.

The coachman gave his horses the office and the carriage rumbled forward at the steady pace suitable for negotiating the London traffic. Colin suddenly felt his throat go dry. While it would be rude to drink lemonade at this moment, he was glad he had asked Mrs. Simpkins to prepare a flask of the drink. He might surely need it—*soon*. Despite their obvious attraction to each other, his conversations with Nora were awkward. He replayed his proposal several times in his head. He felt no regret for their betrothal. She was unlike any other woman he had known. She challenged him to see things from a fresh perspective —her perspective. And he delighted in finding out new things about Nora—and made it his mission to learn everything about her. His head filled with curious thoughts—concerns for children he had never considered existed. He had known of the base-born children littering London's streets, of course. His father had repeatedly schooled him on the cruelty and irresponsibility of spreading his seed in such a manner. Father had brooked no indifference, having no patience for that sort of thing, and had even fought in Parliament to force more attention on the matter.

Sadly, Father had been in the minority. Society knew, but ignored, that the children fulfilled a need, working where small hands and bodies were *de rigueur*, and Colin had himself grown comfortable with that knowledge. However, there were faces now attached to these outrages. He could no longer ignore them. He also had the means to help.

"Did you enjoy the children's lesson in drawing?" Nora's voice interrupted his musings.

"I must confess, I learned much about these children I had never given thought to before." Colin pictured Benjamin cleaning a chimney and swallowed past the small lump that had formed in his already dry throat. "It was... revealing," he managed.

"I noticed you had struck up a friendliness with Benjamin. A woman left him on the front steps a few weeks ago, with nothing but the clothes on his back and a note. An unsigned note, curiously. The child *has* no family, as far as we are aware. He claims to be eight, but I doubt he knows. Benjamin seems small for his age. However, he communicates rather well." She folded her hands in her lap. "He is enjoyable to be with and makes me think," she said. "I suspect it is his gift." She paused. "We all have one, according to my grandmother. Benjamin tells me things and I want to laugh at his presentation of those events, yet at the same time, what he says nearly brings me to tears. Does that make sense to you?" she asked, her gaze holding his.

"He indeed possesses a gift, and what you say makes a great deal of sense. His drawing created a painful reminder of the abuse these children have faced. He climbed into chimneys," he began.

"I had not realized he had been a sweep's apprentice until some days after he arrived. He has a cough," she added, her face drawn. "I am concerned, although there are plenty of negligible reasons for a persistent cough."

"I heard it, too. It could be nothing more than a cold. However, I think it warrants a visit from a doctor. I wonder if you would object to a friend of mine—Dr. Perth—visiting? He moved his practice to London about two years ago from Kent."

"I have heard of Dr. Perth. My grandmother recommends him. She describes his manner as straightforward and comforting." Nora's face colored, and she turned away slightly.

Colin ignored her discomfort, not knowing what he could say to change it. Perth would have found the description amusing.

"*Good.* It is settled, then. I shall have him come to see all the children—unless, of course, you have already done this?" He regarded her, suddenly unsure of where he was heading with this train of thought. Her bright, chocolate brown eyes seemed to smile on their own as she took in the surrounding scenery. Gerard had driven them beyond Mayfair towards Kensington Gardens, an older section of Hyde Park. He had earlier asked his coachman to take a long route through the park, feeling the need to gain clarity with this woman. The more time he had, the better.

"Becca's drawing upset me," Nora interjected. "I could see it troubled you too. Could the man, Mr. Sneed, have been Sneed, do you think?"

"I noticed that. Her picture resembled the description that Aunt Gemma had given of him, and the man that Mrs. Simpkins told us of. "I plan to put a Runner on it. I have already sent word and intend to meet with the man who is in charge of one of the patrols. I am concerned about the dealings, if he was the one, that he might have had with Becca's aunt." *The woman turned up dead.* What was his involvement with Becca? "Her drawing concerned me." He considered his next words. "I will meet with a Runner later today, as I mentioned. I initially planned to have him locate your uncle, but now I feel Sneed needs be found." He had wondered whether to mention that Sneed could be very dangerous and seemed to be a common thread with several of the children, but concluded they could defer the subject for now. There were other, more important matters to discuss. Until he knew more, he saw little advantage to worrying her.

"His involvement in so many children's lives concerns me," Nora murmured, almost reading his thoughts.

"Yes, that was in my mind, too. There are men whose financial existence depends on the backs of children—whom they consider disposable." His instinct told him there could be much more to these men. He decided to speak with Morray as soon as possible.

Colin found he was enjoying this time with Nora. They were already joining in concern for the children, something that he would never have envisioned.

"I have a favorite spot here and thought we might go there today." he ventured, seeking a lighter note.

She smiled. "That sounds perfect. I had hoped we might discuss our... betrothal."

CHAPTER 15

$\mathcal{I}$t pleased Nora that Colin had taken the trouble to select a pleasant spot for their outing, even if it was to discuss the facets of their *arrangement*, although she could not help but worry what the particulars would be.

As a child, she had indulged her fancy over a love match when she married. Yet she had agreed to this arrangement and would see it to the end, resolving to make the best of it. Lord Shefford's interest in the children astonished her—she had not expected that he would truly be interested when he asked to take part. He had been earnest in his request. He had asked nothing mundane and seemed truly concerned about the children's well-being, particularly with respect to Benjamin, who seemed to have gained special favor with the Earl.

"Gerard will set us down and take the carriage and horses to wait beyond those trees. There is not enough room for him to draw up here," the Earl said, stirring Nora from her musings.

"I have never picnicked by a brook before." Nora spoke before she realized her intention. There had not been many opportunities to attend frivolous functions, far less enjoy a picnic. She had worked in the family's mercantile whenever her parents needed her. The store sold all sorts of sundries, including fabrics, notions, and other household items. Since her grandfather's death, her father had struggled to keep the family business afloat. He recently moved his law office to the top floor of the mercantile, and his clients had not seemed to mind. Mother had once commented on the number of new clients found once he moved his office to the mercantile. When she was young, she wondered why Grandmama or Grandpapa had not intervened and helped. As she grew older, she realized pride was a powerful antagonist.

"I find that hard to believe," he answered. "My governess introduced me to picnics as a small child. She would trick me into thinking it was playtime and so I would learn French or Italian while eating the fruits and cheeses she brought along."

Nora liked the way his smile filled his face and his eyes sparkled when he spoke of things that made him happy.

"Did you bring cheese?" she asked. His smile was contagious.

"I did, as well as lemonade and wine. I believe Mrs. Simpkins has packed everything."

"*Both* lemonade and wine?" She laughed. "Not only does she like you, she would do anything for those gifts of sweets."

The groom opened the door. "My lord. I have placed the blanket and the basket on the ground near the water. Please let me know if there is anything else you require." He bowed, pivoted, and went to the front of the carriage, where the driver sat.

"I shall return in a moment," Colin said as he alighted from the carriage.

Two minutes later, the door opened again, and Colin waited, his hand held out for her. Nora accepted his hand and stepped from the conveyance. Once they had walked away from the carriage, she heard it pull away.

"That is lovely!" She stared in wonder at the display before her. A large blue cloth covered the ground between two trees. On the top rested an open basket and two stout pillows—one resting against each of the trees.

"Allow me." Colin guided her to the blanket and gave her time to sit down. She tucked her legs underneath her skirt and smoothed the folds about her.

Nora looked around and noticed, for the first time, that they appeared to be alone. A hint of unease crept up her neck. While she was not uneasy with Lord Shefford, her grandmother would not appreciate having to defray commentary from the *ton*, should they be discovered in this clandestine position. She nibbled her lower lip, suddenly feeling anxious and short-sighted. Perhaps she should have brought Mary along to serve as a chaperone. Yet that would have left Mrs. Simpkins as the primary caregiver with the children. Woods and Marsh would be busy working on renovations on the upper floors. She would simply have to make this a short picnic. There was nothing else for it.

"A penny for your thoughts," Colin asked, rousing her from her contemplation.

"I am afraid I was fretting. 'Tis something I seem to do more of since the orphanage opened," she replied.

"I sense something is wrong. Pray enlighten me and allow me to share in your concerns."

"I daresay I might…" Her voice sounded tentative, even to her own ears. "Would you think me dreadfully ungrateful if I asked you to find a less private place? It is a delightful spot, and in different circumstances, I should love to sit here and enjoy the day. However, if we are discovered here, unchaperoned…"

"Say no more," he said. "I understand completely. I should have given more thought to this. I had been thinking of my own needs— that is, I wanted us to have a place where we might speak uninterrupted. I did not consider your reputation. I know somewhere which might feel more suitable." He turned and gave a quick whistle. Immediately, she heard horses and a carriage moving towards them.

"Gerard, drive on to the lake. There is a pretty prospect close to the palace gardens, with a statue and some benches."

"At once, my lord."

Within minutes, they had collected up the basket and blanket, and returned them, with themselves, into the carriage.

Nora was not sure what to say. She had not meant to create such a stir. They probably would not have been discovered. Anyway, since when did she care what the *ton* thought? She cared about what Grandmama thought, however, and she did not want to create a problem for her dear benefactor.

"Thank you," she whispered.

"Of course! I should have considered. Please accept my apologies. There can be no objection here."

As he finished his sentence, the carriage slowed to a stop. Nora glanced out of her window and saw that they were but a few hundred yards from the Guard's House by Kensington Gardens. Here, the river which formed the Serpentine was surrounded by wide, open spaces. One or two small, empty rowboats bobbed up and down in the water, attached to a small dock beside a boating house. A clump of trees clustered near the bank, and a sandy path led down to a little beach. Logs and the occasional bench on which visitors to the park might sit, dotted the path, each sufficiently distanced. They were not in the main flow of Society, but this north side of the river was a public promenade. They would not be isolated. This was a pleasant prospect.

"This is a lovely spot," she mused out loud, noticing there was no one about apart from a couple walking in the distance. Still, it was more public, at least, so it felt more *proper*. Nora hated that term and found Society's use of it to be hypocritical, at least in her experience. Many of the unwanted children that found their places in orphanages —and worse—had been born on the wrong side of the blanket... a problem created by the *proper* aristocracy.

"Good!" Colin declared jovially.

The groom opened the door. "Will this be satisfactory, my lord?" he asked.

"Yes. Thank you, Gerard," he replied to the coachman. "Give me a hand." Colin nodded towards a small grassy knoll in front of them, and the two men quickly reassembled the cozy picnic spot of ten minutes past. Gerard drew the carriage onto the grass beside the road. He and the groom settled themselves on the box to await his master's orders.

Driven by an uncomfortable growl in her stomach, Nora checked her hat and picked up her reticule, ready for luncheon and conversation. Not waiting for Colin to return for her, she descended from the conveyance and followed the men.

Colin held her hand and helped her sit down comfortably. Before her, a spread of meats, cheeses, bread, and grapes waited.

"Please, take a plate," he offered.

Feeling pinched, she smiled and selected a plate, filling it with the delightful fare, hoping to eat before the embarrassing growl of her empty stomach became an amusement.

"I daresay we should discuss expectations of our engagement," she began, hoping to quell the nervous fluttering in her belly that had added to her discomfiture.

"Things have become somewhat different from the way they were when we first discussed marriage," he said crisply, handing her a glass of lemonade. Nodding towards her glass he added, "I had heard from the children that Mrs. Simpkins makes the best lemonade, so I thought it sporting to try it today."

"How so?" she ventured cautiously, accepting the glass.

As if recognizing her feelings of alarm, he smiled warmly. "Have no fear, my dear. I told you before that I always honor my offers. I have not changed my mind. We will marry." He tugged at his cravat, a sign that he might have felt some uneasiness. "However, I want more."

"Please elaborate, sir," she said, cringing inside and seeking refuge in sipping her lemonade. She gazed at the bottom of the glass as she drank. As she consumed more of the liquid, she discovered more and more clarity. She took the last sip and peeped down at the bottom of the glass. *Now all is clear*. It was an interesting analogy for her life.

It had been her belief that marriages of convenience favored only the men—once his duty done and the calves in the meadow, the bull is free to graze elsewhere. *She* would also be free to *graze*. Had she just used that vulgar comparison? A shudder shot through her as she realized *she had*. A marriage of convenience was not what she wanted. It was exactly what she did not want. She wanted love. She had grown up watching her parents support each other, love each other, and grow old with each other. However, the lives of the children and this orphanage were now her priority. It would secure their future. Grandmama had offered security, but in turn, Uncle Wilford threatened it. Nora needed assurances and marriage to Lord Colin Shefford offered that.

"You must be thirsty," he remarked, nodding to her glass. She blinked.

"Y-yes. I suppose I was," she acknowledged, summoning a smile to turn up the corners of her mouth.

"I was as well." He smirked, picked up the flask of lemonade and refilled their glasses. Nora watched his movements, entranced. His hands were spectacular. They were a comfortable size—hands that could fully enclose her own and keep hers warm. They were hands that could gently smooth away the hair from her face. She remembered his hands holding her, stroking her and pulling her closer.

Some sort of connection between the two of them had developed over the past few days, and she found it hard to disagree with a single thing. *He* had inserted himself into her life, changing everything familiar to her. She shook her head in disbelief. And now, she was engaged to *him*. Her life had turned upside-down, yet she was not unhappy, only puzzled. He was handsome, and despite her initial assessment of him, he was gallant and kind—and very handsome. That point, she decided, could not be accentuated enough.

"Nora." A deep male voice penetrated her thoughts and Nora turned to her betrothed.

"Yes?" Her voice was tremulous. Nora realized she had become so immersed in her musings, she had forgotten what they were speaking about. *Oh, yes, the marriage.*

"I would like to see how we deal together before making any pronouncements about our future life. There is something between us I cannot identify. You are unlike any lady I have ever known, and I find I like you... *rather a lot.*"

"I should, perhaps, thank you for that endorsement," she returned, feeling slightly uncertain over the mixed compliment. "I believe I may like you, as well." Did he mean he wanted to know her better? Perhaps they could gain a more serious understanding of each other? Nora gave a quick shake of her head, realizing she was uncertain of anything where he was concerned.

"Perhaps we should discuss the ceremony. I have yet to speak of this with Grandmama. It will thrill her, of course. It is what she has wanted all my life—something she could not give her own daughter..." She allowed her voice to drift away from the words. She had always understood Mother's reasoning, as she had explained it to her. However, did Nora want something altogether different?

"You are right, of course. We should speak of the ceremony." Colin picked up a small piece of cheese from his plate and nudged it against her lips.

She opened her mouth and accepted the cheese, following it with a sip of lemonade.

"Thank you." Smiling, she pulled a grape from its cluster and fed it to him.

"It is my turn to thank you," he said, edging closer. "Would you mind if I kissed you?"

She glanced about them and saw no one about them. A thrill shot through her body. She wanted his kiss. "I would very much like you to kiss me, my lord."

He placed his hands lightly on either side of her head and leaned forward, feathering small kisses on her lips.

"Mm... your scent is so soft. I think I can detect more than honeysuckle in the fragrance."

To her astonishment, she giggled. "I must compliment your nose, my lord. There is more to my fragrance than honeysuckle. Mother and Father gifted me a bottle to me for my twelfth birthday, and I have worn it ever since. Do you care to hazard a guess?"

"I do." He smiled devilishly. "It does require a deeper investigation, though." His mouth moved from her lips to her neck, grazing kisses along her collarbone.

Warm heat from his breath traveled through the yellow muslin of her dress, causing an involuntary shiver and a gasp of excitement.

"Are you cold?" he breathed, his concern clear, as he cupped her face in his hands and rested his forehead gently against hers.

"Not at all. I am quite..." She grappled for the right word, "...enchanted."

"Is it citrus?" he continued, delicately nibbling her earlobes. "Your fragrance?" he clarified.

"Yes... and one other ingredient..." She exhaled slowly.

"Ah... I recognize... bergamot." He did not wait for her to respond. His lips covered hers in a deep kiss. His tongue swirled the cavity of her mouth, dancing with her own. When he pulled back, she noticed they were both struggling to slow the rapid accent of breath the kiss had stirred.

"That was a... pretty *thank you*, Colin," she said, amused. "I wonder what a piece of meat would have achieved me?"

He roared with laughter. "I have to admit, I rather enjoyed its delivery." A teasing smile lit up his face. "There is such intensity when we kiss." He paused, as if debating his next words. "For a moment, I rather lost my head. I am thus grateful for the privacy we were fortunate to enjoy. Perhaps we should return to discussing our wedding?"

Nora noticed he had changed 'the' wedding to 'our' wedding. Her heart hitched.

"My grandmother will wish to make this a famous event, even though she knows I would prefer to avoid that." Her face warmed as she eyed the basket. "Perhaps a glass of wine would aid our discussion?" She laughed, feeling brighter.

"That sounds like a good idea," he agreed, opening the wine. He took their glasses and poured some wine into each.

"This is quite good." Nora swirled the white wine lightly in her glass before taking another sip.

"My mother will doubtless wish to be involved. I am sure their guest lists will be very similar. Would a larger wedding be so bad if it pleases two ladies we love?"

"I had always envisioned a small, intimate event," she ventured. She started to add something inane, such as her dreams that a prince would scoop her up on his white horse and whisk her off, but swallowed and held her tongue. She doubted he would comprehend such a desire, and she did not want to disturb their growing understanding. "Mayhap, the ceremony can be intimate, and include some of their closest of friends," she conceded, realizing that her grandmother would want to share her joy with her dearest friends. She imagined Lady Shefford would, as well. What Nora wanted was another one of his kisses. *I had never been kissed until he kissed me. Now, I feel almost wanton—in constant need of another. I need more of him.*

"If you feel strongly about the wedding, I will inform my mother of your wishes. I would imagine your grandmother will agree, as well."

"You truly do not object?" she asked.

"I want what you want."

Her heart squeezed at his words. Nora realized she cared about this man. Her heart had become engaged and she was unsure how she felt about it.

CHAPTER 16

*L*ord Wilford Whitton stood hidden behind a large mulberry bush across the street from the orphanage. Wearing a battered, hooded, black cape—apparently unnoticed—he watched a carriage arrive. Two occupants alighted. He recognized his niece, although not the gentleman. The man carried a basket and a blanket and appeared to be dangling after the woman.

Awareness struck, and the side of his mouth curved up in a crooked smile. He studied the two as walked up the steps of the building. Whitton chuckled at his own prowess. He had looked over the entire property, using a loosened board from the tall fence surrounding the backyard as entry.

"It seems my niece has discovered another means of support. I wonder how my mother would feel about her granddaughter's new occupation," he scoffed under his breath. Even saying it out loud, he knew it was just wishful thinking. His niece was as proper and boring as they came. She spurned the *ton* and all that it represented, yet here she was stepping from a carriage. "Her father was too proud to accept my parents' funds when they were offered. Now look at them. She works in an orphanage and her own mother, my sister, works in a mercantile.

"Mother would do anything for her precious Honoria," he sneered. *Out with no chaperone. That's a new peccadillo, even for my hoity-toity niece.* He scrutinized the man's face. Recognition sent an icy chill down his spine. *Lord Colin Shefford!* Instantly, Whitton withdrew further into the bush, considering his next move. *I cannot let him see me.*

Fiend seize it! This complicated everything. His mind unchanged about the task ahead, he studied the landscape, seeking opportunity. A dark movement behind the pale-colored stone building pulled his attention from his niece and her escort. *Lawks! That had to be him. There's been no movement back there for almost thirty minutes.* Still not confident enough, he thought the best option was to wait for Shefford to return to his carriage. Each minute chafed him, and he grew tired of waiting. Most likely he would get no credit for helping, anyway. And he had already spent enough time here. *If I duck behind the carriage quickly, the bushes at the side of the building will cover me.* He looked around and took the chance, moving as quickly as he could until he got to the back corner of the property. At once, he saw him.

His fears confirmed, he knew his niece and her orphanage would suffer if he did not do something—and Mother would blame him. If Shefford is here, I am certain my dear mother knows about my little deception. It sent a sick feeling to the pit of his stomach. He had been naught but a disappointment to her, although his parents had never said a word.

"No, instead she and Father kept the family money from me, leaving me in damned low water. I should not lift a finger to help," he complained to himself. Still, he loved his sister, and he would not see her hurt through Nora, even if his niece's contemptuous attitude galled him.

It had injured his pride when his sister and brother-in-law had refused the opportunity to live at his estate. Truthfully, he had hoped they would maintain it for him. He never seemed to have enough funds and had seen this as an answer to his own need. His mother would credit him for maintaining the estate properly, he had conjectured. His plan had failed.

A tall gruffly bearded man, wearing a filthy brown coat and fingerless gloves, stood from a crouched position at the right front corner of the orphanage and sprinted to the back of the building, apparently still unseen by Shefford's coachman. The coach appeared drawn up for a while, leaving Whitton little choice. He had to take his chances. Checking the door and the coach and seeing no movement, he dashed across the street and stole down the side of the pink brick orphanage. He went quickly and quietly, hoping to catch up with Tom Sneed, although he was not exactly sure what he would do if he caught him. After having stabbed Shefford, Whitton knew he needed to stay away from Shefford's notice. If they caught him, would they believe him?

Whitton reached the back of the building in time to see Sneed leave a spot under an open, second-floor window, before slipping through a second loose panel of the back fence and escaping. Whitton glanced up at the window, and he could hear the sounds of children's voices. He wished he could walk away, yet he had to do something. He had to warn somebody.

Where are the watchmen? His mother would not have placed Nora here without reassurance in her well-being. He had hoped to leave a note for one of them and keep his involvement simple. *So, there it is... plan two,* he thought, vexed. Certain he could reach the loose plank Sneed had inadvertently shown him, Whitton reached into his pocket and pulled out a paper-covered stone. Securing his hood, he surveyed the area. *No one.* Quickly he hurled the stone through a window and sprinted towards the back fence, sliding the loose plank aside and slipping through the gap. As far as Whitton cared, he had fulfilled his responsibility. *I warned them—my conscience is clear.*

"WELCOME HOME, MISS MASON." Woods opened the door and collected her pelisse. "You have a message, miss," he said, handing her a folded note.

A whiff of rosewater met her nose. She flipped the missive over.

Grandmama's lavender wax and rose medallion were as distinct as her scented paper.

"It is from Grandmama. I should look at it in case it is something important. Would you mind?"

"Absolutely not. Please do." Shefford gently nudged her hand.

Grandmama's note said simply that she planned to visit around late afternoon. She could be here at any moment, Nora realized. She looked up and fixed her gaze on Colin.

"May I offer tea before you leave?"

"I would like that," he said, taking off his hat and cape and handing them to the footman.

"Miss Mason, I will ask Mrs. Simpkins to send in the tea. My lord." The footman acknowledged Shefford with a polite nod before heading down the hall to the back of the house.

"I still have much to discuss with my grandmother. Her note said she will be here later this afternoon. I should expect her." Nora's head swam with thoughts of the day. She had discovered her betrothed to be a man who cared about the feelings of others, something she would never have expected. The afternoon had been more than she had imagined. More than she had ever hoped to imagine. Was it possible that they shared the understanding she felt?

A flurry of footsteps could be heard in the hall, ending at the door to the parlor. "Miss Nora, Miss Nora! Someone has just hurled a stone through the kitchen window!" Mrs. Simpkins stood in the doorway, fanning herself and holding a wrapped stone in her outstretched hand while clutching her chest with the other. "I was standing with me back to the window, readying the biscuits fer the oven when this crashed in behind me." She fanned her face with her hands. "Oh, me word! I can barely catch me breath." The visibly pale housekeeper/cook slid into the striped chair near the parlor door, furiously fanning herself.

Nora passed the stone to Colin, who at once unwrapped it. "I have employed a Runner. He should have been at the back of the house, watching. I cannot imagine this happening without him seeing it." He stretched out the crumpled paper. The smudged, wrinkled sheet of vellum held a scribbled penciled message.

. . .

Your children are in danger.

"WHO DO YOU THINK LEFT THIS?" she asked, after reading the note.

"The handwriting looks familiar." He stared at the paper in her hands. "Would you mind if I took this with me? I would like to compare this to something."

Nora assented, and Colin folded the note and stuffed it in his waistcoat pocket. "This concerns me. I had hired a Runner who should have taken up his post. He was to have taken over earlier, from the two footmen. I had hoped he would provide more experienced protection."

Mrs. Simpkins piped in from behind them. "A tall, red-headed man came shortly after ye left and said he 'ad been hired to watch over the orphanage. I saw him head towards the stables."

"Did he give a name?" Colin asked.

"Let me think. I 'ad been helping set up the new boys' room. Mr. Woods and Mr. Marsh finished the room today, you know. The boys, they 'ave a nice new place to sleep..."

"Mrs. Simpkins..." Nora interrupted this prattle without apology. "Did the man give a name?"

"Ah, yes, begging yer pardon, miss. I was just so excited about the new room fer the boys. Let me think. It was a cooking word... give me a minute. I cannot think properly when I get flustered." Her voice cracked as she struggled to recall. Suddenly, she broke into a smile. "Peeling... Mr. John Peeling. I remember, 'cause 'tis an easy name to recall, since I peel carrots and potatoes and whatnot," she announced proudly.

Nora bit her lip to hide a giggle. It would hurt the woman's feelings, and she would never consciously do that. In Nora's estimation the cook could run circles around two women half her age. "Thank you, Mrs. Simpkins. I never doubted you would remember the name."

"Thank ye, Miss Nora. If ye don't mind, I need to see to the evenin' meal and the broken window. 'Tis getting cooler at night and it needs covering. In case ye are in need of her, Mary is upstairs getting the children readied for the evening. I will ask Mr. Marsh to help me." She curtsied and hurried from the room towards the kitchen.

Nora gave a soft shrug. "It seems we never run out of excitement in this house, Colin."

"Yes, I can see that," he concurred.

"The men have added shelving and storage in several of the rooms during the week. They completed Mrs. Simpkins' kitchen first, and she is quite ready to jump over the moon with it," Nora explained. "I am sure she is most upset to see her window broken. According to her, the kitchen was near perfect."

"Be that as it may, if Peeling was doing the job I hired him to do, he would have seen whoever threw this stone and broke the kitchen window. I need to find him." Colin stood there for a moment, pinching the top of his nose. "Something seems very wrong." He turned to Nora. "Would you mind if I asked Woods to help me? We need to make sure the house is secure."

Nora nodded. "Not at all, Colin. Shall Marsh assist, as well?"

"I think Woods and I can cover the back. I would feel better if Marsh remained inside with you and the children."

She pulled a cord in the corner of the room. "Grandmama had this installed. I tried to insist it was unnecessary. Perhaps she was right, though." A moment later, Woods poked his head into the room.

"Did you call for me, Miss Mason?"

"Yes," she responded. "Would you accompany Lord Shefford outside and help secure the perimeter?"

"Certainly, ma'am. I would be happy to do so."

"Good. Come along with me," Colin interjected.

Nora watched the two men leave, feeling oddly safe even after having her window broken with a stone. It was Shefford's presence. Other than her father and grandfather, she knew of no other man who made her feel wanted until Lord Shefford.

"Do you have a sense for what looks normal out here, Woods?" Colin asked.

"Yes, my lord. The footmen you sent to watch the building suggested that I should not only learn the outside of the building but also the interior. They left this afternoon, shortly after showing Mr. Peeling around the orphanage. Come to think about it, I have not seen him in the last hour," the footman said gravely.

"I am regretting having allowed them to leave," Colin muttered, mostly to himself.

The area behind the building had vastly improved under Marsh's attention. Rose bushes provided an additional thorny barrier to the fence on two sides. A vegetable garden was being tilled on the right, marked off with a small, white picket fence. To the far left, a stable large enough to house a carriage and a horse or two stood next to gated access to the cows and chickens they kept in the mews for the daily dairy needs. Behind the stable, they had not cleared an older garden. Rogue bushes stood at the sides and several tall oak trees, in need of pruning, shaded the roof of the stable.

His footmen had been instructed to stay in the small loft above the main floor of the stable. Surely Peeling was not sleeping up there, he thought, irritated with himself. *I should have left at least one footman here.* Yet, with Woods inside and the Runner outside, he had felt that there would be enough surveillance. He feared he had been dreadfully wrong.

"I am going to look upstairs in the loft. Would you check the perimeter, particularly behind the stable?"

"Right away, my lord." Woods hurried to cover the area.

"Peeling?" Colin called out the man's name, annoyed by the lack of response. The carriage bay was empty. "The ladies have this stable, although no means of transportation, it would appear, save going by foot," he muttered to himself. Long, neatly stacked wooden planks lined the rear wall, affirming the projects that Nora had described. He heard a groan coming from the stalls. Carefully, he edged in that direction. Glancing inside the first, he saw a prone figure sprawled across the swept floor. Dashing under the breeching chain, he found the red-headed Runner moaning and trying to regain consciousness.

"Woods!" he yelled, "I have found him." There was blood on the wall of the stall behind Peeling's head, as if his assailant had hit him from behind and dragged him there. His mouth had been stuffed with a blackened rag and his feet and hands were bound with rope. Colin heard sounds of running from outside and moments later, Woods appeared.

"Help me get him to the house," he ordered the footman.

"There is a small cot in the storeroom near the kitchen. We can put him in there," Woods suggested.

"That is a good idea. Did you find anything behind the building?" Colin remembered to ask after a pause, watching as Woods pulled a small knife from his pocket and cut the rope around Peeling's feet and hands.

"Someone had pried loose a couple of planks from the fence. It appeared new because the nails looked fresh. Marsh repaired the fencing early on," he explained.

"Here. I will carry him by his shoulders, and you lift his feet. It looks to be a severe head injury. We need to keep from jostling him too much." Colin recalled being told often enough by physicians that head injuries were dangerous.

The back door to the kitchen opened. "Mercy me! He is bleeding," Mrs. Simpkins, evidently harried, cried out.

They carried him to the small room Woods had described. They had added shelving to the back wall and small jars of preserved items sat alongside baskets of dried spices.

"Mr. Woods," Mrs. Simpkins stated more calmly, "we need to clean the injuries. Could ye retrieve some coal and stoke the kitchen fire? I'll need boiling water t'wash these wounds. It appears he also 'as rope burns where his hands and feet were bound. I can make him comfortable and tend 'is wounds, my lord. And please send Mary to me if ye see her. I'll need her help with this."

"Thank you. I defer to your experience, Mrs. Simpkins. I will send for a physician." Colin was about to find Nora when she appeared at the door to the small room, with Mary behind her.

"Oh, my!" Nora cried as she scrutinized the man on the cot. "Is this your man?"

"Sadly, it is, Miss Mason. I will send for Dr. Andrew Perth, the friend I mentioned earlier. He is very good with head injuries, having trained on the battlefield years ago.

"Thank you, Lord Shefford. I appreciate your thoughtfulness and will be glad of his services." She turned to her servant. "Mrs. Simpkins, please do anything you can. I will see Lord Shefford to the door and be back in a few moments to help you." Her voice trembled. It was the first time Colin had heard any sign of unease from her.

They walked to the front door without a word.

"I will return as soon as I can," he said, drawing her near. "There is no one about..." He could not help himself. Slanting his head, his lips caressed hers, drinking her in. Then he pulled back and cradled her face in his hands. "I think I know who wrote the note; however, I need to be sure. I will send Perth with my driver. And I will make haste."

"Thank you for earlier," she breathed. "Do be careful."

"I will be careful, I promise you." A chill went through him, almost a feeling of foreboding. "Keep the doors locked and have Woods again check all the windows, upstairs and down."

She nodded and opened the door. To both their surprise, her grandmother was standing there, a look of astonishment shaping her features.

"Grandmama!"

"I apologize for leaving in such a hurry, Countess..." Colin began.

"Go, there is no time for delay! I will tell her everything," Nora responded, giving him a reassuring nod that all would be well.

He gave a quick bow. "In that case, I shall return as soon as possible."

CHAPTER 17

*N*ora gave her grandmother a warm hug and a kiss. Grandmama had smelled of violets for as long as Nora could remember, and the scent always soothed her. She needed soothing at the moment. Her nerves were as frayed as she could remember them ever being.

"Let me take your cloak," Nora said, holding out her hands.

The Countess drew back, clearly perplexed. "Where is Woods? I expected he would meet me at the door." She offered Nora her hat, gloves, and pelisse. "I had hoped he would take over the porter's duties. Now I find you assuming the role of butler. The day normally quietens by this hour," she remarked, her speech more succinct than usual.

Nora exhaled a long sigh. "I agree, and it is usually quiet at this time of day. Woods is helping with a situation that has occurred. There is much to tell you."

"Then let us adjourn to the parlor and be comfortable. I always find that a good chair and a cup of tea ease day-to-day upsets," she said affably.

"I shall have Mrs. Simpkins prepare some tea. I want to show you the additional room that the men have completed today. Our little orphanage is coming along so nicely."

The Countess preceded Nora into the parlor and took a seat on the sofa just as Mrs. Simpkins came in with a tray bearing the requirements for tea.

"M'lady, 'tis wonderful to see you. I have served dinner to the children." She picked up a silver teapot and carefully poured both ladies a cup of tea. "'Tis a wee past four of the clock. I would be happy to bring you ladies a light repast to hold ye until dinner," she said, smiling.

"That would be very welcome, Mary. Miss Mason and I have much to discuss. Perhaps a light repast would be appreciated," she said, nodding toward her granddaughter.

"I believe I could partake of a sandwich," Nora agreed.

"Very good, ma'am. I shall return shortly." The maid curtsied and pulled the door closed as she left.

"I rarely need to ask Mrs. Simpkins to do anything. It is as if she knows we need something and appears with it. She is a delight. Thank you for lending her to our orphanage, Grandmama." Nora looked around the room. "We are all quite taken with her, you know, especially the children."

"She is a jewel, to be sure. I was sure she would prove indispensable," her grandmother responded, considering Nora meaningfully.

Nora dipped her head in acknowledgment. "I will endeavor to keep the story short. A man threw a stone through the kitchen window and a Bow Street Runner, who Lord Shefford had engaged to protect the property, was found beaten and out of his senses. Lord Shefford seems to suspect a particular person and left to look into the matter. There is a lot of concern about this afternoon. We do not know whether the person who hit the constable was the same person who threw the stone." Nora bit her lip. She wanted to tell her grandmother about the engagement, which, absurdly, seemed insignificant compared to the rest of the goings-on.

"Obviously there is more, yet perhaps I should begin with my personal news. There is so much to tell you."

"So, it would appear!" the Countess remarked, arching both brows, not bothering to disguise her bewilderment.

Nora stared into her teacup, absently stirring the contents with a spoon. "I have received an offer of marriage." She stole a glance from the corner of her eye to see her grandmother's reaction. To her surprise, the Countess was smiling widely.

"Grandmama, you do not yet know from whom."

"Perhaps I have reacted too quickly. I suspect Lord Shefford."

Nora blushed, bobbing her head slightly in response.

"Not only do I approve, I wish to hear every detail." Gone was all evidence of her irritation at the lack of decorum exhibited by her granddaughter at the front door.

"We began with quite a contentious relationship. You will recall, our first meeting was more or less a notice to vacate the orphanage. Mention of your name gave me a small measure of redress, relief, and a sliver of hope. When he returned, he offered an arrangement. Can you imagine such a thing? He asked that I *show him* that the orphanage had merit beyond the purpose he had in mind for the building." Nora felt renewed irritation at the mere recollection of that request. "I could not conceive the nerve of him. He insulted my abilities, and I refused him. Unsympathetic, I saw how incensed he became in return. Clearly exasperated, he demanded that if he offered marriage, would I turn it down? Out of sheer pique and without proper reflection, I accepted."

Her grandmother's eyes shot open for a second before she tittered, almost dropping her cup.

"I am sure, my dear, your grandfather is smiling from Heaven at you at this moment!" she touched her granddaughter's arm with affection.

"I think Lord Shefford's offer surprised him as much as it did me." She put down her teacup and smiled winsomely at her grandmother. "Of course, he assured me he would stand by his offer. While I am convinced he was duping me, truthfully, his words and honor emboldened my decision to accept. I have no regrets. We seem to rub along well, which I find… refreshing," she said, struggling to contain the heat rising up her neck.

"Considering you have always held little but contempt for the *ton*, I find it ironic that your betrothal makes you a member of Society." A glimmer of laughter glittered in her grandmother's eyes and a satisfied smile settled on her lips.

Nora winced at hearing the truth so candidly, and she recognized when her grandmother felt satisfied.

"We have spoken about the marriage…" she answered carefully, "… today, as a matter of fact. It has been our first opportunity."

"Judging from the urgency in his words as his lordship rushed past me in the doorway, dare I hope that he has developed more feeling towards you and you towards him?" Her grandmother shamelessly prodded for information.

Nora's blush deepened. "I think that is a possibility." She straightened her shoulders and sat closer to the edge of the chair. She had promised Colin she would ask, and at this moment, she had her grandmother's full attention. "I must ask a favor."

"Tell me, my dear. There is naught you cannot request."

Nora studied the Countess' face. She appeared happy, which could prove of benefit.

"Grandmama, I know how much you have wanted me to marry, for as much as it will grant you the opportunity to plan the occasion as a good match would secure my future." She drew a deep breath. "Would you consent to consulting with his mother and sharing the planning of the wedding? It would mean a good deal to him, and he has been so kind to the children, and to me. He is to ask his friend, Doctor Perth, to examine the children. We are particularly concerned about Benjamin, a small boy of eight, who has been here but a short time. He has a horrible cough, and I know he worked in the chimneys before he came to us."

"Are you truly giving me license to plan the wedding your grandpapa and I would have wanted for you?"

"I am but would hope you limit the size of the ceremony," Nora answered, hoping she would not regret this decision. Her grandmother enjoyed creating extravagant affairs.

Grandmama clapped her hands in delight. "It would be my pleasure to take Lady Shefford into my confidence. We are old friends. I find it very thoughtful that you asked. I am assuming I have leave to contact her?"

"Yes. Colin told me she is already aware of our engagement."

"How wonderful." Her grandmother clasped her hands together excitedly. "You and Lord Shefford will form a good partnership. "And I feel there will be much more to this than a mere social pairing." The Countess rose and stepped over to her granddaughter's chair, holding out her hands. "I shall make known to your mother that she and your father should visit soon. I am certain they will be pleased, even with the unconventional offer. The origin of the proposal itself suggests promise. Passion adds spice to a marriage, and to become engaged in a fit of pique is most extraordinary," she added, smiling and angling her head. "Lord Shefford's family is reputed to be honest and generous. 'Tis an excellent match." She sniffed. "And by the way, Dr. Perth is an exceptional choice. He opened his practice in London two years ago and the *ton* accepts him as a doctor of high regard. I would also like to meet this young man, Benjamin, when we review the rooms."

"Grandmama," Nora cried with relief, "how happy it makes me to know you approve! I was worried you would think me too impulsive."

"Not at all, my dear. I understand your temperament well," she responded, her eyes crinkling with amusement.

"If I did not know better, Grandmama, I could almost think you had something to do with this…" Nora let the words die. "I apologize. I know not why I said that."

"Ha! Let me say that if the opportunity had ever presented itself to see my favorite granddaughter married to a man of impeccable reputation and character, I would have tried," the Countess said, once more wearing a knowing smile.

Nora felt a twinge of something. It was the same feeling which came upon her when she had a forewarning. Did her grandmother know something? *No, impossible.* If she did, she reasoned, the Countess would never tell.

Nora shook her head, clearing her thoughts. "Grandmama, have you found anything out about the deed to this building?" She still wanted to know the title's legitimacy, regardless of her promise to Colin.

"I expect to have news soon. My lawyer has quite a few papers to sift through, but he felt it would not take long. I visited his office on my way here, as a matter of fact."

Nora inclined her head. "Thank you. Now, I might tell you of this latest difficulty."

"I have been waiting, although it was delightful to hear of your betrothal first. It has quite diverted me!"

Again, that strange feeling surfaced. Nora studied her grandmother for a moment before shaking her head. *Impossible. What could she have known I have not told her?* Nora took a deep breath and began the tale.

"Lord Shefford and I arrived back after our brief carriage ride. As I mentioned, we were discussing our marriage," she blurted, glancing at her grandmother's face. "Shortly afterward, someone threw a stone through the kitchen window. It was a warning."

"What kind of warning? Perhaps you *should* have told me this first —*not* that your engagement is less important." The Countess's voice trembled. "This portends trouble and I shall want to take some measures to further secure your safety. How was the threat conveyed... and what was the threat?"

"A piece of paper covered it. His lordship and Woods went out to check the garden and stable area, and found the Runner seriously injured. Lord Shefford sent for Dr. Perth," she replied, realizing her response had become more formal.

"Tell me again. *What was the threat?*"

"My apologies. The paper said, 'Your children are in danger.'"

"May I see it?"

She noticed her grandmother's face had suddenly paled. "Colin, I mean, Lord Shefford, took it. He plans to return later."

"My dear, he is your intended. You may use his given name." Her grandmother made a dismissive sound with her tongue and then smiled gently at her. "I would like to see the note, when he returns. Tell me about the injured investigator." Grandmama pressed quietly.

"To my knowledge, he has not yet recalled anything. We have made him comfortable in the storeroom off the kitchen. Incidentally, Woods and Marsh have built some excellent shelving for Mrs. Simpkins. She and I are in awe of their ideas and talent. Thank you, Grandmama."

"I am glad they are here. For the time being, perhaps they spend less time on the renovations until they have resolved this!"

"Yes, Grandmama. I quite agree." Nora planned to speak to them as soon as her grandmother left.

"Shall we go upstairs? I would like to look in on the children. They should be readying themselves for bed now. The boys will use the newly refurbished room, which lies across the hall from the other room, for the first night. I love the small cabinet-type beds the men have crafted on the far wall. It makes more space for beds, without making it crowded," Nora enthused.

"I grew up with a bed similar to those you describe. I would like to see them."

Together, the two ladies went upstairs and looked over the new furnishings. Nora could not shake the strange feeling that had come over her. She did not like the uncomfortable sensation that events were careening out of her control. With the broken window and the injured Runner, she was feeling more and more anxious. When they reached the new boys' room, they found Benjamin in the doorway, staring at the cabinet beds.

"Ah, there you are! Grandmama, this is the young man I wanted you to meet."

Benjamin extended a hand. "Pleased to meet you, your ladyship," he said, bowing.

"Oh! I like him!" her grandmother cooed. She glanced from Benjamin to the room. "Young man, why are you staring at the beds?"

"'Cause I ain't sure I wanna be stuffed in a cabinet. I likes to stretch me legs, me lady, and have more'n one way out."

Nora interceded. "Benjamin, we shall allow each of you to choose. We have a few extra beds in here, if you look." She extended her hand towards the six beds already placed in the room. You may choose your favorite one."

"Thank you, Miss Nora. I want the one nearest the door."

Seeing his apprehension and understanding that it could have something to do with being squeezed into a chimney, she had an idea.

"Benjamin, turn down the blanket on the bed you wish to have. That will signify that you have claimed it."

Excited, he stopped at the bed nearest the door and turned the blanket down. "Thank you, Miss Nora." Happy, he joined the other children, whose voices were coming from what was becoming known as *the girls' room* across the hall. The process to claim the beds had started, and the children were enjoying themselves.

A loud knock sounded downstairs. "That sounds like the front door. It could mean that Lord Shefford is back," Nora said, taking note of her own wistful tone. Colin had not promised to return that day. *He said he would return as soon as possible.* An empty feeling hit the pit of her stomach. She missed him and wished they could have touched once more or had one more kiss before he departed.

"I agree. When he returns, I would like to know more about the message. Perhaps he knows more," her grandmother returned.

They had reached as far as the parlor when Mrs. Simpkins opened the door for Dr. Perth.

"Thank goodness ye are come. The man seems fevered," she exclaimed, quickly ushering him along the hall towards the kitchen.

The doctor stopped at the parlor door and bowed.

"Good day, Lady Whitton. This must be your niece, Miss Mason. It is nice to meet you both. Miss Mason, I will inform you of anything I find."

"He seems to be a nice young gentleman," her grandmother observed as he walked down the hall. "The ladies of the *ton* find him quite handsome. Even without a title, many ladies have singled him out as a prospective spouse." She inhaled, primly.

"I should keep him from Mary's sights," Nora responded with a quick laugh.

"She keeps things entertaining," the Countess responded, amused. "I fear I should probably go home. It is getting rather dark outside. You should go to sleep early, my dear. There are dark circles under your eyes. Please have your Lord Shefford call on me with details of what he finds." She paused. "I do not believe the person who threw the stone meant any harm, based on his message, although that is strange."

"Why do you say that, Grandmama?" Nora questioned.

"To me, the person who wrote the message and wrapped it around a stone, before tossing it through a window, seems desperate. The other person," she continued, "is more concerning. Knocking out a guard takes some calculation, I would imagine."

"You think there could be two men?" An icy shiver skirted down her spine. For the first time in all of this, Nora's unease threatened to overcome her.

"Do you feel unwell, Nora? You look pale," her grandmother remarked, clearly concerned.

"No, Grandmama. I am quite well, although perhaps a little over-whelmed with the day's events. I shall make a point of calling upon you and we can then talk more."

"I should like that very much, my dear. If you will forgive me I shall take my leave." The Countess turned to Woods, waiting unobtrusively near the door, and showed her readiness with a nod. He helped the Countess with her pelisse and handed her her hat and gloves. "I expect you to maintain the comings and goings of this house, Woods. Keep a close eye on my granddaughter and the women and children," she said firmly and loud enough for Nora to hear.

"I assure you, my lady. I have just taken a tour of the environs. The property is secure."

Nora watched her grandmother leave, feeling thoroughly unsettled by her visit.

CHAPTER 18

*C*olin found Bergen at the club, enjoying drinks with Morray. He handed his coat to the doorman who pointed him towards the corner of the primary room where the two gentlemen were sitting, laughing at something one of them had said.

"What has you with such a serious look, Shefford?" Bergen held out his glass in a cheerful toast.

"I am afraid this day has been too eventful by half," Colin replied, accepting a drink from the footman and taking the leather chair nearest Bergen.

"How so?" Morray asked, accepting another cup of hot tea from the footman. He preferred it to alcoholic beverages. No one ever commented on Morray's choice of refreshment.

"I must find Whitton. Another stone was hurled through a window at the orphanage this afternoon. The note appears much the same as the note pitched through my mother's window—just a different message."

Bergen sat up. "May I see it?"

Colin passed it to them and noticed their concern. "I see I do not have to say more," he commented, his voice calmer than he felt.

Morray reached into his waistcoat and extracted a small piece of paper. "I thought you might need this. It is his ladybird's address. We should not waste time."

Colin studied the address. "That is two streets from here. I need to go immediately." He stood to leave on his words.

"Would you like company?" Bergen placed his glass on the side-table and rose from his chair.

"Would three be too much company?" Morray took a last sip from his tea and placed his cup beside Bergen's tumbler.

"I would appreciate the help, if you have the time. There is more to tell. We found the Runner I sent to protect the orphanage with a large crack to the back of his head. It looks serious. Perth should be there now."

"That does not sound like Whitton," interjected Morray. "He is more liable to react to events. And, despite the nasty attack on you, his reputation is one of duplicity, not maliciousness."

"I agree, although that only makes this entire episode more troubling," Colin conceded.

"Let us find Whitton first. He issued what appears to be a warning. He knows something that we need to know," Bergen suggested.

Fifteen minutes later, the three men arrived at a three-story residence on Cleveland Avenue. The tall, shabby pink building at the corner stood in stark contrast to the mostly white ones that dominated the street.

"I assume that makes it easy to spot," teased Bergen.

"The pink building enjoys a reputation based on the lackluster women who live there—not that I have ever frequented this building," Morray added, "However, it has often made my business easier, as I have found many targets of my investigations here." He sniggered.

They took the stairs to the third floor. Four shabby red doors faced the hall, with only a number to distinguish them. They knocked on 3B and a small opening in the top slid open.

"What can I do for you fancy gentlemen?" a woman's voice asked.

Colin recognized the raspy voice as belonging to the woman from the hell. They had the right place. "We would like to talk to you. I will make it worth your while." He held up a gold coin. "Not for your services—for information," he clarified, to Bergen's amusement. The door opened and a woman with reddish hair and a red velvet wrapper stood in front of him, not saying a word. She waved them in and closed the door behind them. Her hair looked like an enormous bird's nest, uncombed and unrestrained. Lip color remained on her mouth and black kohl lined the underside of her eyes. It was obvious they had awoken her.

A bed stood in the corner; it sagged in the middle and was covered with what appeared to be dirty laundry. It was obvious she had slept on top of the linens. The rest of the sparsely furnished room looked dusted and well-ordered—a cabinet, a small table, a chair with a side table, and a lamp. An almost threadbare carpet covered the floor. It was hard to make out anything but blue and pink for the colors. Except for the bed, it appeared she cared about a neat home.

"What do you toffs need?" she asked sharply.

"We know Lord Whitton stays here and we need to speak to him," Morray stated. "I am Lord Morray, this is Lord Bergen and Lord Shefford. We are not here to cause you distress."

At the mention of Bergen and Shefford, her face went pale. "I don't need no trouble. This 'ere's my 'ome."

"We only want information." Colin quickly explained the note, withdrawing the slip of paper and showing it to the jade.

"He did it!" she uttered. "He cares. I knew it."

Unsure of what she meant, Colin noticed her speech was more refined than before.

"We merely need to speak with him. Wait. What did you mean, *he cares?*"

"There was a boy, 'bout eight, what I saved from the chimneys and took to an orphanage. A man overheard me telling a close friend about the boy. He used to work for the cove, see..."

"Doing chimneys?" Colin inquired.

"Tom Sneed is his man and a right villain. A regular brute. Whitton come over furious with me for telling 'im, although like I said, I did not mean to. It just happened. Sneed is awful dangerous, and I be worried about Benjamin."

"You care about the boy." It was more of a statement.

"I do, but I don't have the wherewithal to help him. He already coughs. I wanted to save him—not have him have to make a living like me, doing something he hates…" Her voice faded.

"I know of Sneed," Morray said.

"Thank you." Colin passed the woman two gold sovereigns.

They left and met Whitton coming up the stairs. Colin smashed him against the wall, holding him by the throat.

"Why were you at the orphanage today?" he demanded.

The man's face swelled red from lack of oxygen and he stammered incoherently.

"Cannot breathe," he choked.

Colin relaxed his hold and let him slide down the wall. Crumpled on the floor, Whitton looked up at the men.

"What are you doing here?"

"Do not make me regret not beating you to a pulp. Tell me what you know," Colin demanded.

"I went there to warn my niece. Sneed is looking to make off with some of her children. My visit was to protect her. My mother will be furious if anything happens to her."

Colin angrily cut him off. "You worthless shit. You should have had the ballocks to warn her of this rogue. Instead, you nearly killed my man and threw a stone through the window—frightening the women and children."

No one said a word for a long moment.

Whitton appeared to process the information. "I did not hurt anyone. I only threw the stone. *Sneed did it*. He was there. I tried to find him—to tell him to leave off or…"

"Or *what*?" Colin sneered. "You will throw a stone at him?" He grabbed Whitton by the scruff of the neck. He wanted to hurt him. He felt a hand on his shoulder and reluctantly dropped the miserable excuse for a man. Breathing heavily, he stepped back.

"We need to return to the orphanage," Whitton croaked. "Without your guard, they are in trouble. Sneed is ruthless. I love my sister and even though Honoria is difficult, I do not want to see her hurt."

"We need to stop him before he makes his move. You can help us with his address." Bergen spoke up.

"This is all my mother's fault. If she had not placed me in the position of having to beg for a farthing, I would not be in this situation…"

"Silence! What is his address?" Morray glared at Whitton. "I, for one, am sick of your sniveling."

"He stays at the lodging house behind the hell, near the stable where we… met." Whitton slumped further.

Colin recognized regret on Whitton's face. The man bullied others less fortunate than he, yet he did seem to care about his family—even if most of it was fear of his mother.

The three friends turned, leaving Whitton piled on the floor of the grubby hall.

"I need to check Nora is safe," Colin said as they exited the building into his waiting coach.

"Set me down at the club, if you will," Morray commented as they drove across Town. Send word when you have decided when you want to find Sneed. He is a parasite."

"I will go with you to the orphanage if you do not mind, just in case," Bergen offered. "My horse is at the club. It can stay there for the time being."

"I appreciate both of you. Morray, I shall send word as soon as I have seen Nora and know everyone is well." The coach stopped at the club's Belford Place address and Morray jumped down.

Dusk had given way to nightfall. The doctor had given the Runner laudanum and pronounced that Peeling would recover in a few days. His head would hurt with the ten stitches the doctor had applied to the gash in the man's scalp. Once Perth had left, Nora asked Mary and Mrs. Simpkins to put the children to bed. She had the headache a little, so had taken her grandmother's advice and retired early, yet thoughts stirred in her head. *She missed Colin.*

He did not return, as she had hoped. Surely, he would be here tomorrow? The other two women had the same idea, according to a comment Mrs. Simpkins had made. There were no more sounds of children. *They must be asleep.* She closed her eyes and tried to make herself go to sleep.

A scraping sound, coming from the direction of the boys' room, dispelled those efforts. She sat up and tied her robe, deciding to investigate. Perhaps a hot cup of tea afterwards would help her to sleep.

The room was dark, with only the filtered light of the moon streaming in. *How strange. We never leave a window open at this time of year.* Nora adjusted her eyes and stared into the half-light. There was a figure standing over Benjamin's sleeping form.

"Benjamin, roll away from him! Run!" she cried. The man grabbed her and dragged her to the window. Nora screamed, kicking and struggling in vain as he shoved a dirty rag into her mouth and thrust her onto the window ledge.

"Miss Nora," Benjamin screamed."

The small boy ran to her, pulling at her feet, yelling and finally gaining the aid of the other boys. One ran down the hall for help. Two others tried to help Benjamin pull Miss Nora away. The man reached over to grab Benjamin and was bitten for his efforts. He roared his anger and struck his fist into Benjamin's head, then thrust a filthy sack over Nora's face. She fell limp and slipped over the window ledge. As gravity stole her last chance of survival, her feet followed; barely sensible, she felt one slipper fall off before she succumbed to the cloying darkness.

CHAPTER 19

$\mathcal{N}$ora woke to a pounding head, a freezing room, and a foul odor. Opening her eyes, she saw only blackness and could barely feel her toes. Her feet felt like frozen blocks of ice. She tried wiggling them and rotating her ankles, thinking it might help. She missed one of her shoes and thought she remembered losing it in the boys' room. As her senses adjusted to her mean surroundings, she heard heavy breathing coming from across the room and men's voices filtering up from below.

The sound of something thudding against a wall, she presumed, followed by loud cursing, encouraged her to listen. *Where was she? Where were they?*

"Damn it, Hyde! You do me bidding or ye'll finish yer days slung wi' bricks and tossed to the bottom of the river," a deep voice growled. "I'll say what happens to the wench."

Nora recalled what Becca had said about her mother and shivered in fear. They had found her facedown, floating in the river.

"Yer sure she ain't connected to the gentry, Mr. Sneed? She smells clean," a higher male voice persisted. "She 'jes don't seem like no Haymarket ware."

"Quit yer belly-aching and git her to the game. Wrap her up and git her gone. And never address me by my name if you value yer life."

"Kill me. Ye threaten 'n bluster, yet I knows of none as is mutton-headed 'nuff to take yer coin in trade fer thur soul. I promised me missus I'd not dangle at the end of a rope. Selling a Society miss could make a liar out of me," the second man challenged.

"Do what I pay ye fer. The blonde in the robe will bring more money on the sale table than the other. Make sure ye grab the right one. I want that bitch to pay for interfering with my trade."

"What'd she do, guv'nor?" Hyde probed.

A loud slap sounded. "Damn! What'd ye do that fer?" It was that same higher-pitched male voice. *Hyde*, Nora thought.

"Never ye mind. Yer asking too many questions. Git down there to the tables and tell me when they are ready fer the next one. I need to git to the boys. I have a chimney business to run."

"Yus, yer 'onour," Hyde spat out, the sarcasm evident even above.

Are they discussing me? What game are they talking about? Swallowing a gasp with her fist, Nora realized her eyes had adjusted to the light in the room. It was so cold she could see her breath, and the only thing she had on was her pink wrapper, a gown beneath it, and one pink satin slipper. At least it had a leather bottom. One shoe could not get her far. At least she had not been tied. Perhaps they felt the laudanum had been sufficient.

Nora heard a door slam. It sounded from the room below her. She might not have much time. For a moment, she recalled the dream of a knight in shining armor rescuing her and snorted.

"I had a dashing prince this afternoon. Tonight, I find myself near Hell's door," she lamented. Another snort and a snore reminded her she was not alone in the room.

Something smelled putrid. Sniffing, she leaned closer to the mattress. "Lud, I think something died on this bed. 'Tis nasty," she whispered to herself.

She quickly scanned the room. Boards covered two windows, which had no glass in this mean dwelling. Opposing streams of light pierced the darkness—one from a sizeable crack in the boards covering the window near her, and another from under the door. She scanned the room. There was a broken-down dresser in the corner. It had but one drawer; a second dangled in pieces from an opening. A bed in the corner held the body of the room's other occupant. *One who snores*, she thought. Catching her attention, the moonbeam hit a shining item on the wooden floor in front of her bed. Shards of glass lay everywhere. Cautiously, she bent down to investigate. She had to be careful with only one shoe.

Shivers shook her body, and she tugged her wrap tighter, gingerly extending one foot over the side of the small bed. A squeak sounded, and she withdrew her foot in time to watch a rat run across the room and disappear into the wall. Another involuntary tremor assailed her, and she waited for it to pass. Whether possessed by cold or fear, she had to escape. No prince could find her in this dungeon.

Summoning all her courage, Nora crept to the other bed, carefully avoiding anything that reflected light from the floor, and using the foot with the shoe to clear her path. When she reached the bed, she studied the person lying there. The body belonged to another woman, and a rather bosky one at that, judging from the deep snores and the sour smell of alcohol. There was no telling where they had abducted her from—if there had even been an abduction. The fuddled woman could be up here sleeping off her potations.

Suddenly, Nora had an idea. She pushed aside any inkling of guilt. It could be her only chance to save herself. The woman looked close to her size. It seemed simple enough, but with dead weight, her plan proved harder to put into operation than she had thought. Unsure of how much time she had, Nora tried to stop breathing for long stretches as she tugged the clothing off the woman and replaced it with her own. The clothing stank, but if it saved her life, she would not complain. *At least the shoes fit*, she thought, taking the woman's study boots and replacing them with the single pink slipper. Changing her mind, Nora held onto her slipper. Oddly, the woman was wearing several undergarments, including pantalettes, that looked to have been decent at one time. She refused to wear the filthy undergarment but had an idea. Rolling them up as quickly as she could, she stuffed them into the crack in the window boards. She would need all the help she could create, and eliminating the light would assist that purpose. She stuffed her pink slipper into the pocket of the dress.

A scraping noise on the stairs caused her to abandon switching beds, and she ran back to hers and crawled on to it, turning to face the wall. She gave her best impression of drunken snores and said a silent prayer.

The door opened, and she heard footsteps enter the room. "Damn you, Sneed. This be the last time you tell me what to do. Me missus is right. I'll git me an honest wage from tomorrow. He thinks I'm going to be his lackey. I'm done wi' 'im and his bullying." His footsteps stopped at the bed Nora lay in. "She's still asleep. Won't hurt ol' Hyde if'n I take a little peek." Large fingers grasped her arm. "Huh? What the devil? This don't seem like her. The wench was dressed in a night-gown. Strange, oi thought she were on this bed." The man cursed as he stumbled over something on the floor before reaching the other bed. She heard him roll the blanket around his quarry, apparently abandoning his idea to take a peek. *Thank goodness!*

The man grunted as he hoisted the woman onto his shoulder. "Must be that I'm tired," he muttered. "The wench feels heavier. No matter. This is the last time I'm doing this fer 'im." The door closed behind him and Nora breathed a sigh of relief. Sneed and Hyde. A sense of familiarity pricked her consciousness. She would remember eventually. For now, she needed to find a way out of her prison. First, she needed a weapon. *Where is that large piece of glass?*

"WHAT DO YOU MEAN, she is gone?" Colin's voice bellowed across the room even as bile rose in his throat. Pain stabbed at his heart. Whitton had been right. Sneed had taken her. Perhaps it was a stroke of luck that Benjamin had witnessed the kidnapping. However, the young boy was beside himself that he had been unable to save her. From his incoherent babbling, it seemed that she had saved him. Colin had to find her.

"Mrs. Simpkins, if Benjamin is willing, I would like to see the room and hear the details again, for myself," Colin asked. The women were weeping, and the house was in an uproar.

Benjamin had described the scuffle to the housekeeper and the maid, telling them a big dark-headed man had snatched Nora from the window. Something was missing. He needed answers. He scanned the room, hoping for a clue to her whereabouts. Fresh scrape marks marred the new paint of the recently painted window. Hanging in the inner branches of a large oak tree next to the open window swung a knotted rope.

Woods was leaving to inform the Countess when Colin's carriage pulled up before the orphanage. He asked the man to deliver a message to Morray and have the Earl meet him in the East End, at the lodging Whitton had described. He was sure Morray would under-stand the location. He planned to search there, first.

Nora Mason's ability to manage the intricacies of running the orphanage astonished him. He felt sudden shame for having belittled her on the occasion of his first visit and made a mental note to make up for that somehow. The parlor reminded him of her—and of how he had diminished her with his bumptious offer. Shefford reminded himself that it was her grandmama who had convinced him to make that offer. He owed her a debt of gratitude. First, though, he needed to find his betrothed.

Loneliness crashed in on him. *He missed her.* It felt like more. Did he love her? He had never loved a woman before. Even having his best friends with him did nothing to ease the emptiness. He had never felt this way about a woman.

Benjamin appeared in his nightrobe, holding onto Mary's hand. "My lord, I tried to get him to sleep. He insists he knows where Miss Nora was taken."

"I should like to speak with him. I will make sure he goes back to bed," Colin promised, crouching down so he could be eye level with the boy.

"M'lord, I know where he took her. He brings the women to the Table."

"The Table?" Colin had never heard of it. Was it another hell?

"A bunch of men pay money. I heard him discuss it once with his man, Hyde, while I was in a chimney."

"Where is *this Table?*"

"He called it *the Tunnel.* Said the drunk toffs practically never see their pockets cleaned.

At that moment, the door to the parlor opened, and the Countess sailed in, followed by Bergen.

"Where is my granddaughter?" she demanded.

"Benjamin thinks she is in a place called the Tunnel," Colin said. "Bergen and I are on our way."

"What is the Tunnel?" the Countess insisted, closing her eyes and biting her lower lip.

Colin recognized the same look of fretfulness that he had seen on Nora.

"Take me with you, m'lord." Benjamin's small voice pierced the silence. "I know where the Tunnel is. I want to help find Miss Nora. She saved me life." He reached into his pocket and pulled out her pink shoe. "This fell from the window when he took her."

Colin looked at the slipper. It was delicate and pretty, just like the woman who had worn it. "May I?"

Benjamin nodded and handed the shoe to him.

"Nora will be angry, yet I am fairly sure this orphanage has no way to contain him unless we lock him up. Take good care of him," the Countess interjected, sniffling. "Bring my granddaughter home... please."

Less than an hour later, Colin's carriage drew up in front of the same hell where he had been not more than a sennight ago, except this time he and Bergen had a young boy of eight with them. Colin gave a silent prayer that the boy knew where Sneed had Nora.

"Wait here, m'lords. I must jaw with my friend, Danny." Before they could say anything, Benjamin shot off towards the back of the stable.

"Imagine what it took to bring us back here," reflected Bergen.

"When all this is over, I would like Lizzie to meet Nora. I think they could become friends."

"I would like that too," Colin said absently, fingering Nora's shoe in his pocket. He wondered how long it would be before Morray arrived.

Benjamin returned to the coach with Danny close behind. The two men recognized him immediately. "Danny and I learned pick-pocketing together," he said stoically. "But that was afore Danny found a place 'ere. I also 'elped out here, afore Tom Sneed bought me from the owner of the hell.

"Excuse me? You were owned?" The truth suddenly dawned on Colin. No wonder Sneed wanted him back. Benjamin was one of his cutpurses. And knowing this child, he was good at whatever he tried to do. The man considered Benjamin his property—it was a common enough occurrence—and he was losing profits with Benjamin's disappearance. Colin also recalled the story about little Amy and wondered if Sneed was likewise an opportunist, trying to steal the little girl by posing as her father.

"Yes, m'lord. Me own parents sold me." His voice cracked as he related his sad past.

"We will discuss this later, Benjamin. First, we need to find Miss Mason. Danny, have you seen Sneed?" The thought of these boys being sold distressed Colin, although he would have to consider what he could do about it later.

"'E went in the main 'ouse earlier," Danny offered.

"The Tunnel sits a floor beneath it, m'lord," added Benjamin.

"I think we should start where he lives. Benjamin, where does Sneed live?" inquired Bergen.

"Follow me. I know a way to get in with no one seeing you," the small boy told them.

"Danny, I have a friend who should arrive here shortly. His name is Lord Morray. Will you send him to where we are going?"

"Yes, m'lord. I will bring him to ye," the boy agreed.

The three of them crossed a narrow, cobbled street behind the stable, keeping to the darker side of the structure and avoiding light.

Benjamin led them, stopping at the edge and signaling they wait. He approached the building and tapped on a red, paneled door. After a minute, when no one answered, he signaled for them to follow. They went through the door, climbing dark dusty steps which were lit only by a single wall sconce in the corner of the first-floor landing.

"This is how they bring people into the building for the Table," the boy explained.

A knot formed in Colin's throat as he imagined Nora being carried through this filthy passage. He dearly hoped they would find her here and not in the Tunnel.

A LOUD COMMOTION stirred Nora to wakefulness. *Dear God! How did I fall asleep? I have to escape this room!* While she waited for her eyes to adjust, an argument flared up from somewhere beneath her.

"'Ow did you get the two wenches mixed up, you stupid fool?" a loud voice demanded. A loud crack sounded as if something large had hit the wall.

That had to be Sneed, she mused.

A tiny, nervous giggle escaped her when she thought of the reaction of the roomful of men when they unwrapped the drunken trollop.

"Yer lying. Oi checked, and it were the right one, Mr. Sneed," a second man answered.

Nora recognized Hyde's voice.

"She 'ad the robe and all," Hyde added.

She heard what sounded like a door burst open and smash against the wall.

"Who are you?" Sneed yelled.

She could not make out the conversation but heard struggling and a loud crack, followed by a loud "Umph!"

Thinking she was in untold and added danger from whoever that was, she steeled herself, deciding the window would be her best hope.

Finding a loose board, she pulled at it, hoping to pry it free. *If I can move a couple of these planks, I may escape through the window.* Recalling the dangling drawer, she retrieved it and used it as a lever under the loose end of the board, ripping it from the window. She tried the one above it. Success! Luckily, the commotion below covered the noise she made.

Satisfied with her efforts, she looked outside and saw what appeared to be some sort of stable with a brightly lit building in front of it. There had to be help in that direction. She glanced down at herself. She could no longer smell her own body and imagined she resembled a common strumpet—not that she had ever seen one before today.

Heavy footsteps, from what appeared to be several men, sounded outside the door. They were coming towards her. She had run out of time to escape. Alarmed, Nora grabbed the large shard of glass, no longer concerned with cutting herself. Summoning a prayer, she moved to stand beside the door, holding the glass above her head, ready to strike. A few seconds later, the door opened. Afraid to look, Nora squeezed her eyes shut and brought the glass down. At the same moment, two enormous hands caught her arms.

Fear and hysteria overcame her, and she began to shake and scream. The two hands securing her wrists pried the glass loose and pulled her close.

"Hush! Nora, 'tis me, Colin." He pressed a warm kiss on her forehead.

"Colin?" She was still shaking from fright. "How did you find me?" Tears ran freely, followed by loud sniffs.

"Be at ease, my love. We shall soon have you away from here." He pulled off his coat and wrapped it around her.

"We?"

"Oi came to help, Miss Nora," a small voice beside him answered.

Nora recognized Benjamin at once. "Benjamin! What are you doing here? Why are you not in bed?"

"Oi wanted to help find you…"

Realizing the little boy had helped in her rescue, she pulled him into a hug, cutting off any further speech.

"We must leave. Now." Lord Bergen's voice sounded from behind them. "Danny is guarding the carriage at the door. There are a dozen angry men rioting in the main room—just feet away from the door. They are shouting something about a substitution made in the Tunnel." His mouth curved in a knowing smile. "Morray has secured Sneed and his accomplice for the magistrate—trussed up and tied in a small stall in the stable. He and his men will watch them and make sure neither villain escapes justice."

Nora's head swarmed with questions as Colin hastily ushered their small group down the long staircase and out through the door that opened into the alley below. He quickly placed her on a leather seat inside the waiting coach. Benjamin climbed onto the seat opposite her. She saw Colin give the boy called Danny a handful of coins before joining them on the carriage. As they approached the stable, she recognized Lord Bergen's voice and heard him and Danny drop from the rumble seat. She felt immediate relief—almost elation—once the carriage started again. *I am safe!*

"Thank you! I feel like a princess rescued from a tower—a very nasty one," she whispered hoarsely.

Colin gave a sly smile and tugged her closer to his side. "Did you have something to do with a *certain exchange* that caused a riot in the Tunnel?"

A chuckle escaped her. "I may have had something to do with it," Nora admitted timidly. "I tried to save myself."

"Remind me never to underestimate you again, my darling. I did so once before and I vow never to allow it to happen again," he said with a chuckle.

"I beg your pardon, sir! When would that have been?" she asked demurely.

"Impudent minx! When I challenged you to prove the orphanage to be more worthwhile than my project. However, had I not persisted, we might not be betrothed."

"Very true…" Tired, she laid her head on his shoulder, no longer caring how she smelled. All she cared about was that *he* was here. He had saved her. *Just like my dream… my dearest dream!*

The coach rumbled faster than normal over the cobblestones, tossing the three of them uncomfortably on the bench seats.

Noticeably relieved when the carriage turned onto a smoother road, Colin drew back and lifted her chin with his finger.

"I have a big question," he said, grinning broadly.

He slid from the seat next to her and balanced on one knee. "I do not think I presented my proposal correctly the first time." He cleared his throat and held on as they rounded a bend. "Will you do me the honor of becoming my countess?"

She had to be dreaming. Unsure of whether she really wanted to wake up, she reached up and scrubbed at her eyes. It felt real. She blinked. It looked real. Tears welled up and crested on her eyelids. "Yes, sir, I would love to become your countess."

Colin cradled her face in his hands, his eyes snaring hers.

"Nora, you have made me the happiest of men. When I discovered you missing, my world tilted. I could think of nothing but finding you." Not waiting for her response, he kissed her, at first feathering her lips before leaning in for a deeper kiss.

As if remembering, of a sudden, they were not alone, Colin pulled back and reached into his pocket, withdrawing a pink satin slipper.

"I brought this along to remind me of you. Benjamin found it by the window."

Smiling through her streaming tears, Nora peered behind Colin at Benjamin, who sat wide-eyed and quiet.

"You may both see the humor in this," she teased. Reaching into the pocket of the slattern's skirt, she extracted her other slipper and delicately shrugged one shoulder. "It did little good to have one. I am afraid I sent the other woman to the tunnel without shoes." She considered the gentleman and the boy in front of her. "I am the luckiest person to have two men who care so much for me. Thank you, Benjamin, for helping to rescue me, and thank you, Colin, for making me the happiest of women!

EPILOGUE

ora checked the looking glass above her dressing table once more and adjusted her headpiece. She felt like a princess in her gown. She and her mother settled on an elegant, pale pink spotted muslin dress with a train. A stylish, shimmering gold-pink ribbon separated a one-piece bodice and skirt. Short under-sleeves of white linen added form to the long muslin sleeves, which ended at the elbow. A shimmering over-dress of the palest pink gossamer she had ever seen covered the bodice and skirt. A small tiara of pearls and tiny diamonds was carefully woven into a loose chignon, with her blonde curls softly framing her face.

Absently, she repositioned a stray curl and stared at the image looking back at her. So much had changed in her life in little more than a month. Today was a day she had never imagined possible. She was marrying her own prince—the man who fulfilled that wistful dream of fairy tales placed in her head as a child. This was her day—her wedding day and the day she moved to her new home. Colin had already given her leave to redecorate anything she wished to. She learned that Grandmama had offered another building to repay her uncle's debt, but he had refused it. Uncle had been arrested. According to Colin, the deed to the orphanage had not been the first document that he had altered. At least one more had surfaced, although she had not heard the details. Father was helping Grandmama get it all sorted.

Colin's younger brother, Jonathan, had located the perfect property for their fencing salon quite by accident. With Colin's backing, their dream would soon become a reality.

Her betrothed had made no demands of her, instead telling her to decide about her life and her duties, new and old. That raised him above any gentleman she knew, save her sweet father.

With Grandmama's agreement, she had already established a reduced presence at the orphanage. Mrs. Simpkins and Mary had proven themselves quite competent with the children, and they adored their duties. With the new headteacher she and Grandmama had hired, her own duties would be more supervisory. Miss. Britthaven brought a wealth of experience, and remarkably, shared their philosophy, having once been an orphan herself. Nora planned to use her newly-gained status to influence the ton and follow her dream to raise funds for orphanages. She envisioned working with her Grandmama to establish at least two more in the East End.

True to his word, Colin made sure that Doctor Perth visited the children, especially to check on Benjamin's cough. The doctor had initially worried that the boy might have sustained permanent damage to his lungs. Yet upon thoroughly examining him, Perth determined that exercise and a tonic for the cough would, in time, clear the ailment from Benjamin's system, which was welcome news. Had his time in the chimneys been much longer, the doctor said the lung damage could have threatened Benjamin's life. Uncle's ladybird had probably saved the young boy's life, Nora contemplated. Her grandmother had been so delighted with the news, she offered to help Doctor Perth find a building for his office closer to the orphanage — an offer the good doctor readily agreed to take.

A gentle knock at her door signaled it was time to go.

"Are you ready, my dear?" Her mother stepped into the room, followed by her father. The years had been kind to Lady Eliza Mason. Nora's mother looked young enough to be mistaken for Nora's older sibling. Translucent skin, rich auburn hair with naught but a trace of silver, and a youthful figure still turned heads.

"It means so much to me you could be here. The wedding is happening so quickly." Nora reached over and hugged each of her parents. Her father's law practice, together with the management of his father's fledgling business, gave them little time to be away from home. To her relief, the hard work was finally having the desired result. Her parents' financial straits had eased. Father's pride impeded her grandparents' ability to help them, yet Nora knew her grand-mother took every opportunity to direct business in their direction.

"Your sister and brothers are with your betrothed in the church. They have done nothing but speak of Colin and how wonderful he is. I am afraid we may have difficulty persuading them to leave with us." Her mother chuckled.

Lt. Peter Mason pulled his daughter close. "We are all happy for you, Norabelle."

She felt comforted by her father's use of his pet name for her. "Thank you, Father." A small tear worked its way down her cheek. She had missed his hugs. Nora's father stood tall and looked trim for his age. He was the type of man who commanded attention from all the women in the room when he entered, even though it was obvious he only had eyes for her mother.

"Daughter, nothing could keep me from seeing you marry." He cleared his throat. "Tell me, does Lord Shefford treat you well? 'Tis not too late to back out. I would stand by you." A slow grin quirked his mouth.

"Thank you, Father, but you need not worry," she returned, feeling the warmth of a faint flush tingeing her cheeks.

"We are so pleased you have found a love match, Nora. It worried me when Mama told me you were betrothed. We wanted you to marry for the right reason—love. Having seen you together, I can see I worried needlessly," her mother said, planting a kiss on her cheek.

A furious blush heated her neck. "We have not spoken of love, yet I feel my heart is engaged." She took a deep breath. "Colin looks at me the same way Father looks at you." She had expressed nothing thus to her parents in her twenty years. Nora bit her lower lip, discomfited and uncertain of their reaction.

"He has not mentioned his feelings?" Father queried, sounding surprised.

She dipped her head. "Not yet," she smiled. "Yet, the things he does for me... I feel sure he shares my feelings."

"Fear not," her father rejoined with a slight smirk. "Sometimes the man's brain is the last to resolve these things." He glanced from her mother back to Nora. "Are you ready, my dear? We should not keep them waiting too long."

"I almost forgot. I have something for you." Her mother withdrew a black velvet box from her reticule. "It would mean so much if you were to wear this. I wore these pearls on my wedding day. They were my grandmother's."

Nora wondered what Grandmama's reaction would be when she recognized them. She was certain there would be tears.

"Thank you," she breathed, turning the delicate necklace over in her hand and running the pearls through her fingers. "They are lovely, Mother," she whispered, leaning forward for her mother to attach them.

"There," her mother said, softly touching the strand of beads and stepping back to admire them. "You look perfect."

Peter Mason extended his arm for his daughter. Proudly, Nora accepted it, placing her fingers lightly on his arm, reveling in the feel of having him there to help her brave her way through the ceremony.

The small family arrived at St. George's Chapel in time to see Grandmama and a small convoy from the orphanage arrive. Fourteen children followed her into the church, all outfitted in new suits and dresses. Nora inhaled a deep breath at the sight of all the carriages. She sent up a prayer that she would make it through the ceremony without creating undo attention. Their wedding had become the *ton* event she had feared. She had given her word. Her mother's only wish had been to help with her dress. Nora could not be happier with the selection. The pearls looked perfect against her gown.

As she walked down the aisle, she focused her attention on her betrothed. He stood next to Jonathan, a tall man who bore a striking similarity to Colin except for his blond hair.

The ceremony was a blur until the Reverend called for them to recite their vows. Colin placed an emerald and diamond ring on her finger. As he slid the ring down her finger, he looked into her eyes.

"I know this is but a token, but I hope you will accept this ring as a sign of my affection. I love you, Lady Shefford. Marrying you has made me eternally happy."

Tears clouded her eyes as she looked from her finger to his face. "I love you, Colin. I had never thought to find my prince—until I found you." She lifted onto her toes and placed her arms around his neck as his lips covered her own.

As they walked towards the door, he leaned close to her. "There is one more slight surprise, Lady Shefford."

"What could that be, Lord Shefford, when everything I need is with me at this moment?"

"I will tell you when we reach our carriage." When they arrived at the conveyance, four of the children stood beside it, waiting—Alice, Amy, Becca, and Benjamin. Benjamin stood next to his new 'uncle' Jonathan, proudly dressed in a black coat and pantaloons, with a gold Paisley patterned waistcoat.

"They are all ours, now." Colin beamed.

"Mama... ." The smallest of her children smiled up at Nora with her hands arms outstretched.

"Her first word!" Filled with sudden emotion, Nora picked her up and nuzzled her with kisses. "Oh, Colin, I am so very blessed," she said through her sudden tears, giving each child a hug and a kiss. "I would never have asked you..."

"You did not have to. I know that leaving these children behind would have been too much to ask—even for me. I asked them if they would care to live with us and be part of our family and they accepted. We will give them the love every child deserves."

"Where will they stay while we are gone on our honeymoon?" A moment of concern assailed her. She could not send them back to the orphanage when they had just found a home.

"They will stay with me," her grandmother's voice declared from behind them as she moved closer. "My dear, you make a beautiful bride." Grandmama feathered her fingers across the pearls. "I am so pleased you wore these. I have not seen them in years. They were my grandmother's too, you know."

Nora pushed back tears as she hugged her grandmother close. "Thank you for everything you have done for me... for us," she said, swiping at her tears and smiling at her suddenly large family. "This has been a perfect day, Grandmama." She saw her parents and three siblings approach and waved to them. It thrilled her to see them.

"We will see everyone at my mother's house. For now, I intend to have a few minutes alone with my new bride." Colin pulled her close and whispered in her ear, "We should hurry to the wedding breakfast, so we can the sooner disappear..."

His warm breath elicited a giggle she could not contain.

Benjamin raced to the carriage and stopped in front of the door. "Allow me to open the door for you, *Mother and Father*," he said haltingly as he opened the door. He tried out their unfamiliar names, speaking in the King's English with only a hint of his accent. He had obviously been practicing hard for the occasion. "Would you mind if I rode with Uncle Jonathan to Grandmother's house?"

There could be no better gift from her husband than these four children. Nora reached over and hugged her little gentleman. "I am sure your Uncle Jonathan will take good care of you. Off with you, now!"

"I will be happy to," Jonathan answered. "Do not take too long." With a grin, he tapped Benjamin on the shoulder and the two of them walked to his chaise.

The door to the bridal carriage closed as it lurched forward. "At last, I have you to myself," Colin said, leaning in to give her neck a soft kiss. "I meant what I said a few minutes ago. The night awaits us, wife." He cast a sly look at her.

Nora had never felt so happy in all her life. "My husband, I cannot wait to learn all you have to teach me," she said coyly. She placed her head on his shoulder and peered up at him, letting herself sag against him. Her body pulsed with an unfamiliar need. She was not hungry for food.

"Impudent wife." He cupped her face in his hands. "This will be the shortest wedding breakfast in history… I promise."

He leaned closer and his lips gently feathered a trail of warm wet kisses down her neck as she inhaled his delicious bergamot scent. His slow, gentle nibbles to the lobe of her ear sent delightful pulses to her core and prompted a groan of need. As if in answer, Colin slanted his mouth over hers and kissed her in a way that left no doubt Nora had found her prince.

I hope you enjoyed
EARL OF SHEFFORD
Make Mine An Earl Series
Book 3

**Please consider leaving a review
and/or rating on Amazon.**

Happy Reading,
Anna St. Claire

P.S. Keep Reading for a FREE PREVIEW of
EARL OF HALSBURG
Make Mine An Earl Series
Book 4

FREE PREVIEW

EARL OF HALSBURG ~ MAKE MINE AN EARL SERIES ~ BOOK 4

LONDON, ENGLAND ~ DECEMBER 1826

Disgusted, Alan Hardin, the third Earl of Halsburg, stared at the note he had just received in the morning post. It was the second time in as many weeks he had received one—but this one elevated his concern. "Travers," he called out, stopping the bespeckled, lanky butler as he passed the door to his study.

"Do you recall who left the correspondence with no return name or address?" Alan asked.

"No, my lord. I found it on the top step this morning—only an hour ago."

"I see. That will be all," he said, dismissing the butler, before a thought hit him. "Wait," he said before Travers could take a step.

The butler turned back to face him. "Yes, my lord?"

"Did my uncle ever inquire about a note such as this, one that arrived so . . . mysteriously?" Hardin asked. This was the second such note Alan had received in the past month—and in the year he had been an earl, he realized. The first note he had kept but didn't take seriously. But a second meant someone was determined to make a point. *But what point?* This note bothered him, and he planned to find out who had sent it.

The butler stood for a long moment, perceptibly giving serious thought to the question. "Now that you inquire, my lord, I recall there was a time such a note arrived. It was a month before the carriage accident. I know that because we had a footman to start that day, and I had been training him when he stopped me. He asked me if I knew who had left it, much as you have. It, too, was delivered before sunrise. I believe he mentioned his plans to contact the magistrate, but I cannot be sure. However, he asked me at the time to have his solicitor come to see him."

His uncle's death had been an accident. The magistrate said the horses had been spooked and, as a result, the carriage flipped, trapping his uncle beneath the wreckage. "Did the magistrate ask you questions after his death?" Alan asked.

"No, my lord. The only time he visited was to alert us of the accident and the earl's demise," the butler returned, his response coming slower and more introspective than it had been.

The management of the estate had been thrust at him, so Alan ran things much as his uncle had run things, including his solicitor, so he used the same firm as his uncle had done, including using the same legal firm. "Send word to my solicitor that I wish to see him," Alan said, staring at the note. "Let me know when he plans to come. Also, have the room my mother enjoys using prepared. She plans to be here this week."

"On that, my lord. Her ladyship sent word yesterday evening from the coaching inn that she expected to arrive later today. Her note indicated only that she would want a . . . hot bath upon arrival."

Had sweat appeared on Traver's upper lip at the mention of his mother? Hardin bit the inside of his cheek to keep from smiling. His mother was certainly a force of nature. While she treated his servants as her own, she maintained civility; therefore, he felt no reason to intercede. She didn't interfere with his life, and he gave her free rein when she visited. "I trust you to oversee her arrival and see to whatever she requires." His uncle had rarely entertained, and Alan allowed the servants to go about their business, rarely causing a ripple in their day. But when his mother visited, all that changed. The townhouse hummed with activity.

"Yes, my lord." The man turned to leave, but turned back. "I alerted the housekeeper and sent the cook to the market this morning to select the special foods your mother prefers."

"Thank you, Travers," Alan said, glancing once again at the note before looking up. Mrs. Nimble and Mrs. Canary knew exactly what his mother required. "That is all." He would find out what they had discussed. His experience as a spy for the Crown told him this was too coincidental and worth investigating. A niggling concern surfaced with the timing of his mother's visit, but he pushed it away.

"Yes, my lord," Travers said.

"I want the outside of our house watched round the clock. Assign a footman to watch the front of the house. Hire two more if you need the staff. Not only do I want a report on whom you plan to hire before you offer the position, but I wish to meet them as well. Make sure you investigate their background thoroughly. This is the second such note that has been delivered. I want to know how and who is delivering them—and the need for security became heightened with this second one."

The butler brightened, perhaps glad to have something to do other than please Alan's mother. "Yes, my lord. I will see to it."

"I look forward to seeing your selections. It needs to be done immediately, so make it your priority," Alan added.

When his butler left, he reached into the desk drawer and withdrew the first note he had received only weeks earlier, placing it side-by-side with the latest one, comparing them. The handwriting appeared identical, but he doubted that helped. Both letters were hand-printed in what appeared to be an attempt to conceal the sender's identity. The message on this second note was as direct as the first:

You should not be the earl...

The first note had been more circumspect, and while he had not discarded it, he had not felt alarmed by it. This second one, however, drew alarm.

Fraud! Why did you inherit?

Alan was not a happy man as he mounted the granite steps of 276 Bedford Street to meet his friends. One look in his eyes foretold his black mood. He had accepted the earldom but had not been pleased. A year ago, life had seemed so orderly. He had returned from a Crown assignment, only to be told his uncle had died suddenly and that he had inherited an earldom—something he had never coveted. Additionally, he became the guardian of his uncle's best friend's daughters. Not something he expected or enjoyed. Up to now, he had signed off on anything his solicitor recommended. The one meeting he had held with the girls' stepmother, Baroness Rollins, had not gone well, forcing him to remind her of his position. She had a reputation as a greedy woman and an unpleasant one at that. He planned to keep their dealings short and had asked his solicitor to pay the modiste and other vendors directly on the daughters' behalf, instead of giving it to Lady Rollins.

Christmastide would be upon them soon, and he was glad he had agreed to his mother's London visit. He needed to reconnect with his wards and thought his mother would enjoy helping with the two young ladies. The eldest was twenty and the other fourteen; at twenty-five, his age gave him a decided disadvantage, at least with the eldest. She was as attractive a woman as he had ever seen. An oval face framed by thick, russet-colored hair and green eyes. *Or were they hazel?* He closed his eyes, determined to shut her out of his mind. After the first and only time he had met her, her image had haunted his dreams.

He would be her guardian for less than six months. *Surely, I can maintain my priorities and be the guardian she requires.* In that vein, a recent bill from a local modiste left him with questions about the baroness and his charges. It seemed the young ladies might get *short-shifted.* He needed to think creatively about this guardianship and felt his mother's presence might provide the answer.

His solicitor's visit earlier in the day had been arduous. Mr. Penman confirmed his uncle's death had been listed as an accident, and he confirmed his uncle had contacted him about a similar note a few weeks before his death. Since the circumstances of the carriage accident looked cut and dry, no investigation had ensued. But after today's note, and Alan's discovery his uncle had also received a similar one, Alan wondered if it had been an accident. Since no one had investigated Uncle Edward's death, evidence that might have proven something to the contrary might prove difficult to uncover. Alan had the power and resources to investigate, and as a trained solicitor himself, he recognized slapdash work by investigators. Beyond annoyed, he wondered if he had inherited not only an earldom but also a target on his back.

As if that wasn't enough, his solicitor had complained about the welfare of his wards, two daughters of the closest friend of his uncle, who had died six months before his uncle—Miss Elizabeth Rollins and Miss Penny Rollins. This only added to his suspicion that things were not going as he had hoped. The report about his wards had been unexpected, but in this, he planned to garner his mother's help. Perhaps it would distract her from her unrelenting reminder that he must marry and secure the future of the earldom. Alan hoped her focus on the girls might give his household a much-needed break from her scrutiny.

The large, nondescript townhouse blended with those around it. Except for its red door marked with a *W*, it looked no different. Alan knocked at the door as he fingered the small gold 'W' insignia on the pin anchoring his neckcloth. It was a modest emblem, but every member was required to wear his when in attendance. He had been presented with the pin a year ago, following his induction into the club.

While the club was not in the most fashionable district, it compared favorably with White's, but only with the richness of its interiors. The walls were papered in either deep burgundy or hunter-green tones throughout, and the lighting was low. Only the most masculine furniture—rich leathers, dark wood grains—appointed the club's public rooms. The membership used the club as both a meeting place and a den of pleasures—depending on desire or need. Alan resisted the seedier aspects of the club but found it an excellent place to relax and meet with friends.

"Lord Halsburg, welcome,"

"Thank you, Stewart. Two friends plan to join me for a drink. I'm sure you recall Lord Shefford."

"I do. He was a member a few years past."

"Yes, Shefford will have his brother, Mr. Jonathan Nelson, with him. Nelson's the proprietor of the new fencing club, *En Garde.*

"I understand, my lord." The older man's lip twitched, but he maintained his haughty demeanor. "Your friends await you in the club room—they are seated near the fireplace."

Halsburg quirked his brow. "Thank you, Stewart." He felt his mood lifting, despite the feeling the cards had been stacked against him. "Have someone bring me a brandy."

"Yes, my lord. Right away."

"Shefford, Nelson," he said, shaking their hands before taking the empty leather chair beside them. "I'm glad to see the two of you and could use some advice."

"My lord, your brandy," a footman said, approaching from behind and placing Alan's brandy on the small table beside his chair.

"If you want to ask about marriage, I highly recommend it," quipped his best friend, Colin Nelson, the Earl of Shefford. "I just need to find someone to tempt my brother here into settling down."

"I'm tremendously happy for you and your lovely countess. However, marriage-minded mothers are one thing I have not enjoyed since attaining the earldom. While I have no immediate aversion to marriage, I find the cloying debutantes and their mothers tiresome and avoid them at all costs," Alan said, chuckling.

"Colin's about to wear us all down with his perpetual cheer these days," said his brother, Jonathan Nelson with a laugh. "I can, however, attest it hasn't taken the edge off his fencing. My customers ask to fence with Colin, perhaps because of his newly gained master's status."

"Please, don't . . . Jonathan," Colin said, swirling his drink and turning a slight shade of pink. "It was a requirement for opening the club—we needed two masters."

"That makes good sense. I've heard good things about the club. How's it been doing?" Alan asked. The brothers had opened the fencing club to honor their father's influence in their lives. Both men were considered fencing masters, a title only given to the most accomplished. "If you'd like to expand, I would be an interested investor. *En Garde* may do for fencing enthusiasts what Jackson's has for pugilists."

"That's a nice offer and we will keep it in mind. The club has been a tremendous undertaking, but Jonathan operates it carefully, which has been tremendously beneficial for everyone," Shefford replied.

"It's been in great demand among the *ton*," Jonathan agreed.

"Our fencing training was helpful during the war. Has that affected admission applications?" Alan asked.

"Yes, we've seen a lot of interest," Shefford said.

"And I hope it stays that way," Nelson bantered.

"I'm glad our venture has been successful. But that isn't why you asked to meet," Shefford said.

"I'm in earnest about becoming a silent partner, so if you decide to pursue expansion, speak with me." Alan's face became pensive. "You are right, though. I need your advice. I've gotten two notes—strange ones questioning my legitimacy as heir."

"How could that be? Your father—your uncle's only brother—predeceased him, and your uncle was without issue," Shefford put in.

"Exactly. And if that wasn't strange enough, I discovered this morning my uncle had received a similar note—delivered with no one seeing who left it—shortly before the accident. I can only guess what they wrote but, without finding it, I have no way to know. It seems coincidental," he said, withdrawing the notes from his pocket and passing them to his friends, "but pertinent."

Shefford read the notes and quietly passed them to his brother.

Jonathan looked up after the second note. "Same person wrote it. It certainly would be helpful to have the note your uncle received. Have you sorted through the office to see if it's still there?"

"I hadn't thought of that," Alan admitted. He'd begin looking immediately. Perhaps Travers would remember if his uncle had mentioned anything.

"If your uncle received something similar and died in a coaching accident that wasn't investigated . . ." Shefford began. "You may have a target on your back."

"My thoughts exactly," Alan said.

"It somewhat takes the shine off of being elevated to the peerage," Shefford said.

"Yes. It does. While I don't see how that can be changed, I don't plan to have my life snuffed out over primogeniture. I plan to find whoever is sending the threatening notes to me," Alan said.

"What can we do to assist?" Shefford asked.

"You've heard me out and don't feel I'm off track. That's tremendous support. I sent a note to the palace before I left the house, requesting an audience with the king's agent. My father died, and outside of my younger brother and myself, there were no other males. But I'm wondering about the transition *before* my uncle's inheritance and need to investigate. If someone has a question, that might be where we find them," Alan conjectured.

"The king's agent's name is Ruben—*Mr. John Ruben*," Nelson said. "I contact him frequently with applicants at our school when there are questions. The last thing I want is for our school to gain notoriety for a bad actor who uses the skills we teach them dissolutely. "I'll put Ruben in contact with you."

I hope you enjoyed this FREE PREVIEW of
EARL OF HALSBURG.

Make Mine An Earl Series, Book 4

Tempted to read more?
You can find it on Amazon.

Happy Reading,
Anna St. Claire

HEART TO HEART

Dear Reader:
You are cordially invited to join my Heart to Heart Community.

Get the inside scoop on upcoming releases including the next Make Mine An Earl book.

Plus sneak peeks, freebies, contests and more.

No spammy stuff.
Only yummy stuff.

Join:
Anna St. Claire's Heart to Heart Newsletter
And get a *Noble Hearts Series Free Preview*!

Or you can visit my website:
annastclaire.com

Happy Reading,
Anna St. Claire

ABOUT THE AUTHOR

Who knew I'd become an author? Not me. But when the opportunity came, I grabbed it and approached it like I've done everything in my life—celebrating the hits and laughing at the misses. Nothing worthwhile is easy, and that includes everything in my life. But I have much to smile about—a beautiful daughter, two precious granddaughters, my adorable dogs, and my sweet husband of over thirty years. He has always supported me—including uprooting to move to the other side of Charlotte, N.C. for a life change, just when we thought we were *settled*.

If *settled* means nothing changes, then it'll never describe me. I give everything to things I enjoy—and that includes writing. In 2021, I hit the **USA Bestselling Author** list, and recently, two of my favorite books were named *RONE* **Finalists**!

My daughter avoids crowded movies with me because I'm *that woman* in the row in front of you who gleefully munches her popcorn and laughs at every hilarious scene. Loudly. Besides my family, I love chocolate, popcorn, laughter, and animals. To keep memories of my pets alive, I frequently sprinkle them in my stories as secondary characters. British and American history has always interested me, so writing historical romances in those genres always excites me.

When I was barely three, my mother moved my sister and me from New York to the Carolinas. Juggling a full-time job and full-time school, my mother became my first genuine hero—never waving the flag when things were tough. Things quickly got tough. My grandmother, who taught me to read before I started first grade, died before I was seven and I've never forgotten her.

Margaret Mitchell's *Gone with The Wind* remains one of my favorite stories, but Kathleen Woodiwiss' books, Shanna, and Ashes in The Wind, hooked me on historical romance and the dream of writing.

While I primarily write Regency romance, I enjoy almost any period in American and British history.

Connect with me via my website: www.annastclaire.com
Email: annastclaireauthor@gmail.com
Or on social media.

BOOK LIST

MAKE MINE AN EARL SERIES

EARL OF WESTON
BOOK 1

EARL OF BERGEN
BOOK 2

EARL OF SHEFFORD
BOOK 3

EARL OF HALSBURG
BOOK 4

NOBLE HEARTS SERIES

THE EARL SHE LEFT BEHIND
BOOK 1

ROMANCING A WALLFLOWER
BOOK 2

THE DUKE'S GOLDEN RINGS
BOOK 3

MY LORD, MY ROGUE

BOOK 4

SILVER BELLS AND MISTLETOE

BOOK 5

SCANDAL BENEATH THE STARS

BOOK 6

NOBLE HEARTS BOX SET

EMBATTLED HEARTS SERIES

EMBERS OF ANGER

BOOK 1

OTHER TITLES

A WIDOW'S PERFECT ROGUE

ODDS ON AN EARL

THE DUKE'S GOLDEN BELLE

www.ingramcontent.com/pod-product-compliance
Lightning Source LLC
Chambersburg PA
CBHW020437180626
46812CB00003B/1288